A Minor Happy Ending

An Ever After Novel

SHAAN RANAE

Shaan Ranae

A MINOR HAPPY ENDING

SHAAN RANAE

A Minor Happy Ending

This book is a work of fiction. Names, characters, places, and incidents are the product of the author's imagination or are used fictitiously. Any resemblance to actual events, locales, or persons, living or dead, is coincidental.

Copyright © [2016] by Shaan R Hess. All rights reserved, including the right to reproduce, distribute, or transmit in any form or by any means. For information regarding subsidiary rights, please contact the Author.

Edited by TCB Editing

Cover Design by: Jessica James

Manufactured in the United States of America First Edition

Shaan Ranae

Table of Contents

Prologue	vi
Chapter 1	1
Chapter 2	7
Chapter 3	14
Chapter 4	19
Chapter 5	27
Chapter 6	30
Chapter 7	33
Chapter 8	40
Chapter 9	45
Chapter 10	50
Chapter 11	53
Chapter 12	61
Chapter 13	64
Chapter 14	78
Chapter 15	85
Chapter 16	95
Chapter 17	100
Chapter 18	111
Chapter 19	118
Chapter 20	129
Chapter 21	139
Chapter 22	151
Chapter 23	156

A Minor Happy Ending

Chapter 24	168
Chapter 25	174
Chapter 26	180
Chapter 27	187
Chapter 28	196
Chapter 29	203
Chapter 30	208
Chapter 31	218
Chapter 32	225
Chapter 33	229
Epilogue	235
Dedications	240

Shaan Ranae

Prologue

"Just go, you fucking liar." Are the words I hear while sitting on my back porch reading my next love affair. Deep mumbling sounds of frustration ensue, I hear a high pitched squeal, "Just fucking go, we're done! It's over! Leave!"

On that note, I rise from my comfortable chair and quietly walk toward the noise to find a young couple in a lover's quarrel. Two stubborn people don't equal an easy going relationship, but I can tell they care about each other. I watch as he jumps in his car mumbling a few sad words. Not quite sure what he says, but his shoulders slump, his eyes fill with tears as he drives off. After I can no longer see his tail lights, I watch as the willowy girl drops to the ground in a fit of sobs. Waiting for a second to let her calm down enough to edge the embarrassment, I slowly walk up to her. She must register my approach, because she turns with a jolt and her eyes narrow. With venom she spits out, "How long have you been listening? Never took you for a

A Minor Happy Ending

eavesdropper, mother!" With that remark, I know she must be really hurting. She's never spoken to me like that. I reply gently in an attempt to lighten her mood, "Well baby girl, I was reading about my latest book boyfriend when a crazy amount of loud profanity interrupted and I thought 'oh hell that should be more fun to watch!'" A small smile displays on her lips, "Always the smart ass!" she says, small sobs escape her, drawing me closer and wrapping my arms around her. After rocking her on the ground for a few minutes, we decide that it's time to take it indoors. "Mom?" she says as she stands and walks into the house. "Yeah, baby girl?" I whisper reassuringly. "He lied to me! I absolutely hate being lied to more than anything!" I knew that to be true. "What did he lie about?" I ask, hoping to allow her to vent her feelings and give her some piece of mind. "It's actually what he didn't tell me, that's still lying!" she says with vehemence. In all of my years, I have been lied to many different ways, about many different things, and they all feel like a betrayal. "What didn't he tell you?" I ask gently in hopes that I can get a clue of what's going on. She replies quickly, "No offense Mom, but you and Dad have the perfect relationship. I've barely ever heard you guys fight. You always say that he is brutally honest with you. So, what wise words do you have for me now?" Ouch, she definitely is my daughter with that sharp tongue. I need to remind myself to send my mom some flowers. Whew! "Well, daughter of mine, your dad wasn't the first man I've ever been with or my only love." Her eyes widen and I continue, "but he is the love of my life." She states, "Right mom, I know you were pretty and had tons of guys after you blah..blah..blah.. I doubt you guys fought like we do. I mean it's all the time. We are either fighting or kissing. It's like there is no in between. We are both crazy jealous, it feels like he doesn't trust me sometimes. It seems like we are more obsessed with each other than in love." Little does she know how familiar that sounds. I had a love like that, obsessive, hot, and passionate. One minute you were all over each other, the next you were at each other's throats! Yep, that was me and Jace. "Trust me, baby girl. I know more about that than you think." I hold her as I reminisce about a time of encompassing passion, my first love.

A Minor Happy Ending

Chapter 1

It was a brisk evening in early June when I found myself sitting on Cam's porch, waiting for my friend Max, as usual. We were heading to The Diner, our favorite late night haunt. In our small town of Apple Creek, there weren't too many late night spots, so The Diner became the hang out. The Diner was what I called a "po dunk" restaurant. Kind of like an old mom and pop place that had killer food, a comfortable atmosphere, and the night manager didn't mind squatters; since it left the late night drunks without a place to sit. Plus, I worked there and got a sweet discount. My friends spent quite a bit of time there, so it was kind of our place. Plus, The Diner had the best pancakes north of the Ohio river, which I had a serious craving for right now. Gosh, Max, what was taking so long? I shrugged my shoulders gesturing to Cam my frustration.

Cam was short for Cameron, she was tall with dark brown hair. She was well spoken and a little spoiled. She was a typical party girl who was new to our happy little clan. She came from the more upscale part of town, after graduation she was eager to start out on her own away from her family. We met Cam at The Diner late one night while sipping coffee and having totally inappropriate conversations. Ever since, her tiny one bedroom apartment had become the stomping grounds for our clan as well as her friends from school. Her house was basically party central. Most of us were new grads, eager to let go for our first summer as adults. She was one of the most fun people to party with, well, with the exception of me.

    In school, my friends and I were the quiet ones. We received the honors by day and became a rowdy bunch, at night. We've had our wild rendezvous that we disguised as sleepovers at my friend Jade's house. Her mom was never home or was having a party of her own. Her mother never suspected a thing, because we were always hiding down in Jade's room, drinking and sneaking in boys.

Jade was the youngest, but acted like she was the most responsible. She was always trying to be the voice of reason, it seemed like all that accomplished was more drama. In my opinion, she was addicted to the drama. It was like she couldn't live without it, but in the end she was

A Minor Happy Ending

one of the most loyal friends a person could have. She had long strawberry blonde hair that hung all the way to her hips and honest hazel eyes. She was probably the polar opposite of me, but as friends, we complimented each other well.

Then there was Max, sweet, naïve, and totally vulnerable Max. Jade and I were always protecting her from herself. She would give a crack addict a pipe if he asked her for one and she would feel that she did him a favor. She had long dark brown hair from the recent dye job I gave her. It needed to be done, since the hot pink just didn't fit her skin tone at all. Thin, but not skinny with a chest that a playboy model would've paid for. That girl would seriously have back problems one day. Her pale green eyes always seemed a little sad. She was the most open minded and impressionable of us, but we couldn't tell her that. She got so angry at Jade and I when we'd try to protect her. Which was why I was sitting on the front porch waiting on her to go to The Diner while my friend was inside with God knows who, smoking a joint.

As Cam and I sat there waiting, we were accompanied by an awkward silence, which usually happened when we were together for too long. You'd think since we were similar that we'd never had a loss for words, but she and I were usually competing for something. Actually, I'd always had this feeling that she was trying to replace me in my tight nit group of friends. She always seemed to cause some sort of drama, but Max and Jade liked her, so I put up with her for them.

Max finally came out of the house with her eyes glazed over, she was in a fit of giggles. Her pale green eyes were so watered and zoned. It made me wonder how much weed she smoked. She smelled like she bathed in it. I guess we needed to drive with the windows down to air her out. Her petite frame looked like she could topple over with that large chest of hers and her coordination was terrible. When she smoked, I would worry, I'm afraid she would either topple over or get molested. "Easy there babes, ya ready to head to The Diner?" She slowly raised her head to acknowledge me and asked, " Yeah, ya want to go get Nick?" appearing sincere, but annoying me with her question. Nick's her brother. He was tall with light brown hair, same shade of pale green eyes and toned body. He was as sweet as Max. Oh, and did I mention he was my boyfriend. "Nah, let's just make it a girls night," I replied. It wasn't that I didn't like Nick, he was great, but my boyfriend's shelf life usually didn't last longer than a couple of months. I was trying to be more careful with Nick because of Max. She nodded and her smile reached her pale green eyes, agreeing that a girls night out sounded good. I'm excited. I enjoyed my girl time.

Turning toward Cam and Max, "ya'll ready to go?" I asked

in the best fake southern accent that I could muster. "Let's do it," Max said with a giggle, we all sauntered toward my little Buick Century. I know, not a badass car, but it got me from point A to point B.

As I opened the driver's side door to get in, Jace Harvey stepped out onto the porch and yelled out to us, "Hey, where are you guys headed" he asked in his sexy drawl. I yelled back, "The Diner, ya want to come?" We'd met a few new friends through Cam, but only one had etched their way permanently into my brain. Jace Harvey, OOOOOOOOOH Jace Harvey.

Jace was beautiful. He was tall with short blond hair that was just long enough to tug on. Mystical dark blue eyes that made you want to take a swim in them with long curly eyelashes, only a woman could be jealous of. WOW, his smile. A full set of lips surround his perfectly straight teeth that sparkled when he showed his signature crooked grin. He had a broad chest and muscular arms, not creepy body builder muscular, more toned. I am not totally sure, but I thought I saw some ink creeping up from the top of his shirt. He was totally hot, but he didn't see it. He was even a little shy. He'd been friends with Cam since elementary school. They seemed to have a love/hate relationship. They argued a lot, but I saw the friendship there too. So, maybe Cam wasn't all that bad. I knew drooling over another man while dating my best friend's brother was not a good idea, but my body just pulsated when Jace was around. I was totally aware of any movement and sound coming from him.

From the back seat someone muttered, "I'm sure he does." I assumed it was Max, because Cam was working her way into the passenger side door. I wasn't sure how Max felt about Jace, but I was wondering if she could sense my attraction to him. In the meantime, Jace yelled back, "Sure I'm starving!" and hurried to the car. Jace jumped in the backseat with Max and I heard her whisper, "So much for girl time." As I looked in the rearview mirror to assess her mood, that was when I saw his sexy smile grow as he met my eyes in the mirror. He knew that I had a boyfriend, so I doubt that he'd attempt anything. I had my suspicions that underneath this all American boy was a bad boy in disguise.

Chapter 2

When we arrived at The Diner, we found our usual crowd awaiting us. Jade was there sitting with her cream cup full and a little coffee added (a private joke between us). Smith, the guy she claimed to have a serious crush on was with her. Smith was sweet and shy. I met him at The Diner when I started working there as a waitress a few months back. He was an artist. He sat there all night drinking coffee and sketching whatever he desired. He was handsome and had a scruffy look to him. His light brown hair and crystal blue eyes enhanced his features. He never had a lot of money to tip, but he always left me a rose made out of napkins every time that he sat at one of my tables. Jade was an artist too. She was so gifted, she was planning on attending the art institute in the fall. So, I guess I saw the attraction with Jade and Smith.
Our little foursome entered the dining room, the hostess Barb commented, "Dyllan, you are always here, don't you have a life other than The Diner?" She was usually perky

with customers, but she had never taken a liking to me. Barb appeared to be a sweet old grandma type, but I was pretty sure a tiger lied underneath. She was very guarded and only associated with certain people, which was fine by me. I didn't think we'd get along too well anyway. I wasn't too upset, I had never even bothered to talk to her other than out of necessity. " Well, since I've met most of my friends here and that's where they are, I guess not." Max and Jace chuckled behind me while she scowled. Cam just lead us to our normal table and ignored my poor manners. She continued with her agenda to flirt with Smith in front of Jade just because she could. I slid into the booth expecting to have Max slide in beside me, but instead I decided to lean back and attempt to knock her out of the booth. I enjoyed messing with her when she was stoned. I leaned into something hard and I felt a jolt of electricity through my entire core. My face began to warm and I felt the blush on my chest. Oh my God, I purposely rammed my body into Jace. Our eyes met, my heart began beating faster. "Oh sorry, I thought Max was sliding in," I stuttered, feeling like such a jerk. "No harm Dyl, nothing wrong with a pretty girl touching me." Jace said with his shy smile. I felt the blush rushing up my neck and in my ears. Hopefully it didn't reach my cheeks, oh God please don't reach my nose! He'd think I was a distant cousin to Rudolph. "Um, okay," I replied shyly and completely out

A Minor Happy Ending

of character. As this was said, Max stared at me as if I was growing antlers. "What?" I said exacerbated. "Nothing," She said equally annoyed with me. Jace just looked at both of us like we were a couple of cackling chickens. "Max, I don't think you're mellow enough, pretty girl. Ya, probably should've smoked s'more." Jace said chuckling, lightening up the mood a little. As Max smiled, I felt a little ping of the green eyed monster sneaking in. I didn't even understand why I was jealous, he just called me pretty girl too! Also, I already had a man sitting at home waiting on me. The last thing I needed to do was repeat history. I would be good this time. I would be good this time. I would be good this time.

  But Jeesh, the longer I sat next to him, it was deemed a very difficult task. We spent the next couple of hours talking and laughing. Thinking about abstract asinine things since half of us at the table were stoned. Max said trying to be philosophical, "What if the aliens made the pyramids? That shit looks too heavy! They couldn't seriously have the technology back then to make them? How did they get it to be so smooth?" Her comments caused my head to shake and a giggle to bubble out. As the rest of us played stupid head games to pass the time, Jade wanted to play stories, I was great at that game, but just not in the mood for it. So, I just sat by and watched the others. I watched them target people and make up horrific fake tales about their lives.

Even though all that was going on, I noticed that Jace's leg was resting comfortably next to mine, every nerve in my body was on high alert. My whole left leg felt warm with those tingles springing up all over the place. Not the tingles when your leg falls asleep, but the kind that felt like butterfly kisses along your skin. The longer it was there, the more comfortable I was with it there. It felt right. It felt normal, like an extension of me. I wondered if I just sat completely still , if I could smell him all night long without being noticed. I wished I could smell him up close. I was so glad no one had any clue what I was thinking right then.

    Wait- Scratch that!

    I was pretty sure Jace might've known what I was thinking right then since he just leaned in and was resting his hand between our legs. His eyes were trained on me, he was staring at my mouth? He leaned in a little closer, I sucked in a slow breathe to catch one of the most heavenly smells, Jace all Jace.

"Dyl, I can't reach the creamer, can you either lean back or hand it to me?" With confusion in his stare, he continued, "Wow, did you smoke too? Maybe I should drive home?" Jace said with his signature chuckle that not only made me feel like a total dumbass, but brought me out of my self-induced Jace daydream. Embarrassed and a

A Minor Happy Ending

little snarky, I replied, "Well if you just used some manners Ace, then maybe I would've grabbed them for ya." I proceeded to fuel the conversation, "you know, you just wanted to touch me since it's been a while for your cute ass." I glanced over to where Max was sitting and felt like I must've grown the antlers back. As he leaned over me to retrieve the cream, I noticed a slow intake of breathe, on his way back he whispered, "You've got a cute ass too." Shit! Shit! Shit! I glanced around the table, trying to assess the situation, hoping that no one heard what was just said and no one seemed any the wiser. Well except for me, holy heck. I thought I just drenched myself. His breathe, a mixture of sweet coffee, and mint as he spoke in the sexiest drawl I'd ever heard. I had never had this happen before. If that was all he could do to me with six little words, he could probably give me the Big 'O' with the slightest touch. I was in trouble. My body, my heart, and my brain were in a tug o' war, I had no clue which one was winning. My body was begging for Jace. My brain was telling me that Nick was my boyfriend. My heart was telling me that not only would I hurt Nick, but break Max's heart in the process. Damn, that heart of mine won. I had never given a guy my heart, maybe it was because I'd never kept them around long enough or maybe never found one worthy enough.

Shaan Ranae

Regardless, my friends Max and Jade took up quite a bit of space in that heart of mine, I couldn't think of anything that could make me break their hearts. So, I guess heart, you won this time. "Hey guys, I'm getting tired. Are we ready?" I said trying to seem weary and did my best fake yawn in the process. I was not sure if it was convincing, but it worked. We all said our goodbyes and headed to the car. All four doors slam, when I looked into the rearview mirror, the same blue eyes were watching me with what seemed like concern or skepticism. I turned the corners of my mouth up, but it didn't reach my eyes. He smiled in return in, but it was as fake as mine.

The car ride back to Cam's was uneventful. The only sounds were those of the radio for the first ten minutes until Max tried to sing along with the music. She was adorable, but she wasn't a singer. We all laughed and joined in at times with her failed attempt to sing the correct lyrics or hit the proper notes, but that was part of her charm. I loved her for it. As we arrived at Cam's place, she offered us the couch if we didn't want to drive home. "You guys can stay here if ya want. Jace can take the floor in my room and you can crash on the couch together." Max looked at me in question as did Jace. That damn heart, "Nah, but thanks, Nick is waiting on me at Max's. I told him that I'd be over tonight." I said trying to be a great girlfriend. Max said, "Yea I'll just head home

A Minor Happy Ending

too." Cam and Jace left the car, waving as we drove off, but I noticed that Jace looked disappointed. He stared at the ground, looking like someone stole his favorite toy. Cam dragged him by the arm toward the house.

Chapter 3

The car ride was mournful as Max and I drove in silence to her house. I parked in my usual spot to leave room for Nick to get out in the morning so I could sleep in. Max and Nick were not only siblings, but roommates. When their parents died two years back, Nick became the ultimate guardian for Max. He had only graduated the year before and was a diesel mechanic in the next town over. He loved working on cars. When his dad was still alive, they restored old cars and sold them, just to buy another car and started all over again. Nick quickly became Max's whole world and eventually part of mine.
At first Nick just saw me as Max's obnoxious friend, Dyllan. But, I think over time he learned that I truly valued that little goof. If I could hand pick a sister, I would pick Max. Nick never really showed any interest in me until after graduation. After graduation, I spent a lot more time at their place. One night, Max and I began inviting him to

A Minor Happy Ending

hang out to watch movies. Then it continued with dinners, small quaint gatherings (parties), and sleepovers with Max. During those nights, Nick and I would joke, flirt a bit, and talk a lot. Max was always there and involved, well except for the flirting. What could I say, I flirted! That was what I did, honestly I wasn't even sure I knew when I was doing it. What led us to our courtship was one night Nick had come home late after a long day. Max and I had fallen asleep on the couch watching a movie. At some point, I felt my hair being brushed away from my face and the sweetest words spoken. "Sweet girl, wake up and go sleep in my bed, I'll take the couch." I awoke confused as to where I was and whose hands were touching me. Not that I was scared, weirdly it felt like it was normal. When I saw who it was, I just smiled and thanked him as I walked into his room.

When I awoke the next day, he had all ready left for work. So, I didn't get to thank him for letting me crash in his bed. I had to work that night, but Max had asked me to come over after I got off at 2 a.m., I agreed. I had nothing pressing at 2 a.m. When I arrived, she was half awake and I told her that I would call her tomorrow. After I left her room, Nick was sitting on the couch just looking at me. Panic set in. Was he angry that I was at the house that late? As I went to open my mouth to apologize, he spoke first. "Dyl, ..." he paused and sighed so loud that I thought it would wake up Max.

 "What kind of soap do you use?" What the frick was he taking about? He almost looked sick as if he was going to puke? Meekly I replied, "Umm, peach strawberry, not sure about the brand, why?" He replied utterly exasperated, "Because, I can't get you or your smell out of my head, ever since I came home and found your smell on my pillow. I just want to carry the damn thing around with me all fuckin' day. I've been noticing what a beautiful woman you are for weeks, but I can't fall for you, you're my baby sister's friend!" I felt this strange pull to him. I walked with purpose straight to him and kissed him. I kissed him long and hard sucking on that bottom lip, loving the taste of him. What could I say I was a sucker for sweet words. After that, I was hooked on all things Nick, it was almost like I moved in right after that night.

No, I wasn't a total slut, but that was an awesome way to get told that you are wanted. Plus, I liked him. He was sweet, funny, and sexy as hell. I was worried about dating my best friend's brother, but she even seemed excited about us dating, which made me happy in return.

All of our girlfriends had a bit of a crush on him. Who wouldn't he was amazing, which brought me back to why Max hadn't talked the whole drive home.

 After I parked and we trekked it up to the house, we were greeted with those pale green eyes and sexy smile. "There

A Minor Happy Ending

are my girls." My sweet man stated as we came in the door. Max's mood seemed a bit lighter than before in the car, she was smiling again. Max returned, "girls? Really girls? We are grown women now. Did you forget dear brother?" As he snaked his arms around me and squeezed me tight. "And how is MY woman?" he whispered in my ear, it caused the tiny hairs on the back of my neck to stand up. I replied, "I had fun, Max and I hung out at Cam's then headed with her and Jace to The Diner. We ate and drank way too much coffee I may not be able to sleep for a week." He leaned over to whisper, "Well that helps with my plans for you." I felt the heat rise in my chest and the tension in my belly. Damn him and in front of Max! I guess I had been a bit neglectful in the affection department lately. I'd been busy. But he was so yummy when he wasn't trying to be the responsible adult he was so used to being. I knew at times, he still felt a bit weird about dating me since I just finished high school, but we worked.

"Well, we thought about coming to get you, but we thought a girls night was in order." Max blurted out making me feel about an inch tall. "But I thought Jace went?" Nick asked with a knowing smile on his face. He knew Max was being protective of him due to my track record with boys, but he took the bait anyway, DAMN. I defended, "Well it was supposed to be, but then Jace came out and asked if he could join and ya know I couldn't be mean and say no." Nick smiled a knowing smile and said, "Yeah, I know babe, you are just too sweet." He was too good. I knew he was way better than I deserved, but as long as he was mine, I would enjoy. I turned to look at Max, blew her a kiss and said goodnight. I led Nick to the bedroom and after which I'm sure you can figure out what happened, all was right in the world again. Nick was my sweet man, who adored me. Jace was a wet dream who made me want to keep my head in the clouds all day. I wouldn't lose my real Nick for a dream or Max for that matter.

Chapter 4

The next morning I awoke next to my sweet man. Wait! What? Why is he still here? I began to nudge him, trying to sit up, but was weighed down by his chest and arms. "Babe! Babe! Wake up. You're late for work!" Then that sweet smile appeared that I loved so much. "Relax babe," he replied, "I've decided to take the next couple of days off since you don't work until this weekend." Surprised, I exclaimed, "Awe! Good now scoot over so I can go back into my nook." He chuckled at my bossiness and made room for me so I could lie my head comfortably on his chest. As his arms wrapped around me, I felt how happy he was to be home with me for the next few days. His hands began to roam and so did my mind. Flashes of Jace's face entered my mind causing such a distraction, he stopped and asked, "You all right? Where did you go, babe?" I replied, "I'm here, just lost in the moment babe, your hands feel amazing." As long as it was his hands I kept thinking of. As he had his way with my body, until the time we both fell apart, my eyes remained open to concentrate on him and him only.

    That day he made me breakfast. We went shopping with Max and then Nick surprised me, "Hey, how about you finally take me to 'the infamous' Cam's house. I am curious where my girls are going most nights and coming back a little-glazed looking." I replied quickly, "Well, of course, you can." Awe man, I hoped that I totally did not drool over Jace and ruin any chance I had at a normal boyfriend instead of all the douche bags I normally dated . Max looked a little triumphant right now. I hoped this wasn't her doing. Hopefully my best friend had enough faith in me not to purposefully hurt her brother. Not so sure, hmmm interesting?
When we arrived, the usual people were there. Jade, Cam, Smith, and Jace. They were sitting on the front porch smoking and laughing as Max, Nick and I walked up the steps toward them. The gang greeted us with bright eyes and toothy smiles, but Jace's eyes were narrowed with a smile that barely curved his mouth upward. He didn't look my way again. Not even a 'hey pretty girl how's it goin?'- nothing! Instead, he was directing a lot of attention Max's way. Smoking weed, smiling, talking in hushed tones, and making her blush with his signature crooked smile that I loved so much. I didn't think Nick was catching onto my

A Minor Happy Ending

scowls and annoyed behavior, because Cam was more than happy to attempt to be the center of his attention all night long. The sad thing was, it didn't phase me at all. It bothered me more that my best friend had the attention of my wet dream. My wet dream! My crooked smile! My dark blue eyes that I could swim in. Ugh, WAKE UP DYL, a voice in my head said after I noticed I hadn't said a word in a while and everyone else seemed to be having a wonderful time. Normally, I was the fun one, the party girl everyone loved being around. Being jolted out of my personal pity party by Jade, when she said, "What up bitch? You are too quiet, did someone shit in your cheerios this morning?" That was when I said the thing I probably shouldn't have. As loud as I could I exclaimed, "Nah, baby girl" grabbing Nicks arm and squeezing, "This sexy man kept me up all night bringing the "O" over and over."

Nick turned red, but looked proud, Jace would've had whiplash the way he snapped his head to look at me. The look I received from Max as well as Jace was a look of severe disappointment and maybe a little sadness on Jace's part. No, he was just a flirt. He'd been flirting with Max all night, so why was he bothered about something I said. I leaned closer into Nick's side and said, "I'm hungry ya want to head to The Diner? Or we can make something at home?" Nick was quick to agree to The Diner, he knew I couldn't cook and he had to do the bulk of the work. As I was tying my shoes I heard my sweet man, "You guys want to come? I like getting to know my girl's friends." He said as he hugged me close causing me to stumble and almost fall, but by true Nick nature he stabilized me and made me safe. My sweet man! To my surprise, two people spoke up, but not who I imagined. Jade and Jace claimed that they were starving and needed some major pancake therapy. Cam decided to tag along even though she wasn't hungry. Smith said he'd give Max a ride home, so we didn't have to make a special trip. Then the five of us hopped into my Century, Nick slid into the passenger seat and I in the drivers side. That left Jade, Cam, and Jace squeezed in the back seat. Poor Jace was stuck in the middle with his long legs cramped.

We waved goodbye to Max and Smith and headed to The Diner. When I went to check my rearview mirror, I was greeted with sad eyes. I forced a tight smile and received one in return as I felt Nick's hand slide up my leg. He attentively stroked my leg and used his magic fingers to ease my tense muscles. In the back seat, the girls chatted while I couldn't even begin to think of a conversation that I could possibly have had at this moment due to fingers running up and down my legs as blue eyes stared at me through a mirror. All I kept imagining was that the owner of those blue eyes was running his fingers up and down my

A Minor Happy Ending

thighs as he was searching for a way to make me fall apart, making me his and only his.

"Dear!....." as I imagined fingers tickling the inside of my knee. "Yea?" I said half listening. " Dear!......" his mouth following the same path those hands just traced. "Uh huh?" I replied. "Dyllan, DEER!" Nick screamed as I came out of my stupor. A large deer with too many antlers had a spotlight in my high beams. I quickly, slammed on the breaks and swerved to avoid the deer, but caused Jace and I to smack our heads together. "OW, fuck Dyllan! Are you ok?" Jace yelled and half scared me since his voice had never risen barely over a whisper. I replied, "Yea, I think I am." Nick started looking at my head for damage and demanded to drive since I was obviously too tired to drive us safely there. When I walked around to get in the car, Jade and Cam were giggling and making rude gestures about my wild sex night that made me so tired that I almost got us all killed.

Nick had a new nickname after that night. Naughty Nick! Oh My God, those girls needed to get a life. And Jace looked like he needed an ice pack. I turned around and apologized to him repeatedly. After many times of Jace dismissing my apologies and forgiving me quickly, I finally let it go. Nick kept glancing at me every couple minutes; he caught me staring at Jace. As a quick cover, I said, "I'm just worried about his head, I hit it pretty hard." "That's what she said!" I heard in unison from the two crazy girls in the back who had done nothing but giggle since they'd gotten in my car. Nick quickly pulled over to the nearest gas station to get some ice for our heads. The girls followed him in to grab some pops and candy. Jace then got out of the car, he paced back and forth. It was making me nervous, so I said, "Please sit and let me see your head. I know I have a hard head, so it had to hurt." He looked up and attempted to smile, but couldn't quite pull it off. "Dyl, just let it go," he sounded frustrated and half pissed. "I feel terrible, I shouldn't have been daydreaming while I was driving." Then that crooked smile I loved so much came out as he sauntered so close to me that I felt the heat radiating off of his body. Then he said, "It all depends on what you're dreaming about." Oh hell, he knew. Damn verbal diarrhea! Shit, was I that obvious! My face blushed and my whole body heated up. I felt warm in my core and wet between my legs. Damn him! He knew. In an attempt to recover from my embarrassment, "Now, let me take a look at that head of yours." As he leaned in closer so I could reach it, my eyes landed and stayed on his lips. His tongue darted out to wet his lips and that plump bottom lip glistened. I wanted a taste. What would his lips taste like, hmmm I wondered? He whispered, "Dyl" at the same time as I heard "Dyl?" over my shoulder from a familiar sweet voice. I quickly recovered by pulling Jace's head down dramatically and examining the raised red area to his forehead. Nick rushed upon us, thrusted me into his arms and applied ice to my head. I startled and squealed at his abruptness. "Babe, I'm fine. Jace needs the ice, not me." Then Nick said with his eyes narrowed and a condescending tone to his voice, "Oh yea, I forgot. Here," as he threw the ice in Jace's direction. His arm returned to its protective place and at that moment I was glad we were part of the human species. I did not prefer the way other animals marked their territory! At that point, the girls returned from inside the gas station and assisted Jace willingly with applying the ice pack and making comments about how hard my head was. Thanks, girls, I appreciated it. We all got back in the car, Nick drove and we arrived at The Diner.

We had a normal but cerebrally engaging conversation at The Diner that night. Jade was in rare form, cracking plenty of jokes at the expense of my sexual exhaustion and my hard head. Cam of course was the life of the party as usual except her counterpart wasn't able to perform tonight. The strange looks she kept sending my way, when she gestured for my crazy antics and obnoxious comments that I was usually good for, were few and far between tonight. No energy or gumption to be the center of attention tonight. Nick seemed concerned. I grabbed his hand to ease his tension. By no means did I want him thinking this had anything to do with him. This was all me. Jace even attempted a shy smile my way when a completely inappropriate comment about my big "head" was made, which I normally would comment on with a much more inappropriate comment. Man, what was up with me.

Chapter 5

After we've had our fill and dropped everyone off, Nick and I went back to his place. We crept in not wanting to wake Max and got ready for bed. As I brushed my teeth I kept thinking of those blue eyes, I literally shook my head to get them out of my vision. I was with Nick. He adored me, treated me well, and made me smile every day. Why won't those blue eyes stop haunting me? I finished brushing my teeth, washed my face, and made my way into the bedroom where Nick was sitting on the bed with a look of concern on his handsome face. I slowly walked up to him and encased my arms around his neck, as his arms squeezed my waist, pulling me closer to him. He held me so tight I could hardly breathe. He whispered "Baby, do you know how much I love you?" I took a deep breath and exhaled slowly, knowing there might've been another reason he was confessing this, other than he never had before. I responded with a whisper, not exactly knowing what to say, "How much?" Holy crap, I didn't know if I was ready for this yet. LOVE. How did he know? Was he saying this just because he thought I liked Jace? Or did he truly think he loved me? It had only been a couple of months. He was searching my face for answers I wasn't ready to give, then said, "More than you'll ever know. Babe, I know it's only been a little while, but it just feels right. We feel right. You have become the light from the dark in my life since after my parents died. You already love my sister and she already sees you as family." I didn't know what to say. I deeply cared for him, but I wasn't totally sure that I was there yet. Then his voice brought me out of my head, "Babe you don't have to say it back just yet, I just wanted you to know where I stand. I just want to know where you think we are heading. Oh shit, I sound like a girl don't I?" I sighed and said, "Well I guess there's worse things than being loved by a man that is remarkably kind and gorgeous! I hope you know that even though I can't say it yet, I completely live and breathe everything Nick." After those words left my mouth, he relaxed his body and had a gleaming smile that warmed not only my heart, but my insides. What was I doing thinking with my HooHah! I needed to control my hormones when it came to Jace. There were too many people that could be hurt, they were all too important to me. That night we made love, then cocooned ourselves in that room for the next two days. He

A Minor Happy Ending
loved me, I should've been happy. I should've been in complete bliss. Maybe I'd get there soon.

Chapter 6

My first night back to work was a Friday night and we were busy. I barely had time to visit with my friends when they came in and sat in my section. I was just their waitress tonight. The girls were laughing and flirting with random boys that came in. Jade almost talked a couple of the guys into buying their meals until Jace and Smith showed up, ruining the whole scam. Jace and I fell back into an easy flirtatious banter as I took his and Smith's orders.

When I returned with their drinks, I noticed Jace and Max cuddled in the booth talking in hushed tones and smiling. Neither seemed to notice the rest of the world, which should've made me happy for my best friend to have had such a handsome man flirting with her, but it just made me nauseous. I just couldn't understand where this came from. Yes, Max was beautiful, smart, and funny. She deserved someone special that made her happy too, but why Jace? Why the only other man on the planet that I couldn't seem to get out of my head. Although I was still

A Minor Happy Ending

trying! I just needed to bury that little green monster and enjoy my friends' happiness. They occupied each other's time for the duration of their meal and waved goodbye to me as they left. Max called out, "See you at home later?" I responded quickly, "Not sure yet, may need to go home and get laundry done." Max looked at me like I'd grown a second head, shrugged and said, "Well, maybe later then." I nodded.

The rest of the night flew by. I stayed busy and at the close of The Diner, I had made $213 in tips. It was great, but now I had my side work to complete before I went home. I checked my phone and noticed some texts from Nick.

Nick: *Hey babe, Max says you might not come by. Let me know so I don't wait up. I'll miss you, tho. Luv u.*

About two hours later.

Nick: *This really is just about laundry, right? Are you busy or just not texting me back?*

As I was just about to text him back a third text came through.

Nick: *Babe, please don't let what I said scare you away. What we have is good right?*

Man, he was worried.

I quickly texted him back.

Me: *Sweet man, I've just sat down. We've been terribly busy all night and I've made a killing. I miss you too. And yes it is only about laundry, I've been with you for 3 days straight and need to go home sometime and get clean clothes.*

I hit send and within seconds.

Nick: *Come here and I'll wash your clothes. I need you here with me.*

I knew I probably should have said no, but I was a sucker for all things Nick. I texted him back, one simple word to make him happy. *OKAY*

Chapter 7

    I finished up my side work and gathered my things. As I was exiting the back doors of The Diner and inhaling the fresh 2 am air, I saw someone leaning against my car. Cautiously, I slowed my gait to assess the situation. The figure was shadowed, but I could definitely tell that it was a tall, lean male. As the figure paced back and forth, moved in and out of the shadows, recognition set in, it was Jace. He wore his fitted white t-shirt with loose-fitting jeans that hung off of his hips. When he noticed my presence, he stopped pacing, shoved his hands in his pockets and there it was. The crooked grin that I couldn't get enough of. Confused and a little nervous I asked, "Hey, Jace, what's going on? I thought that you left with Max. Is she ok?" While continuing to seem nervous while staring at the ground, he replied, "Uh well, Jade and Smith took her and Cam home. I told them that I wanted to clear my head for a while and then I'd find a ride." I couldn't help but think that wasn't the entire truth. Why would he lie, said that little voice in my head. As I walked closer, I thought that I saw those blue eyes I loved so much darken even more. His breathing became more rapid, he began to fidget as I closed the space between us. It felt like a magnet was drawing us together. Just as our toes touched, I awakened from the spell that was Jace, then I asked, "Hey, you doin' okay? Ya want a ride? I can take you home on my way to Max's," with that comment Jace's face fell. With sad eyes, he said "Nah, I don't think my head is quite clear yet." As he began to sway his legs front and back with his hands in his pockets. He still seemed so nervous. I was beginning to worry about what was bothering him. With a concerned voice, "C'mon Jace, Let's take a drive and you can tell me what's bothering you. Let me call Nick and I'll let him know that I'll see him in the morning." and he complied. I called Nick but no answer, so I left him a voicemail that I decided to head home after all and will see him tomorrow, followed by a text message that said

Me: *and it's not about anything but laundry! Night*
Hopefully, when he woke up and saw the messages, he would understand. It wouldn't hurt to spend one night apart. Plus, I was only eighteen. Playing house at a young age might cause permanent damage.

After my messages were left, Jace and I entered the car in silence. As I turned out onto the road, I noticed Jace's breathing had evened out some, he seemed slightly more

A Minor Happy Ending

relaxed than when we were at The Diner. He began to fidget with the radio when an classic alternative song began to play, he left the song playing about half blast in my car. I looked in his direction with my peripheral vision to catch him doing the same. I began to laugh as his shy chuckle joined my laughter. We continued to just drive in silence, sneaking glances in our periphery. He eventually broke the silence after about twenty minutes. "Thanks, Dyl," he said in a whisper from those sexy lips I repeatedly dreamed of nibbling on. I just nodded patiently hoping he'd stop being so vague and give me a hint on what was bothering him. I could just ask, but I didn't feel it was my place. So, I began to sing along when a rock ballad filled my speakers. That song always put me in a good mood, it was definitely one of my guilty pleasure songs. As we drove and I sang, I finally saw a gleam in those blue eyes that gave me the ego boost that I needed. He finally spoke, "Well now that my ear drums are busted, let's find something else more suitable for you my tone deaf friend." I acted shocked and openly blushed, then said "Wow, what a gentlemen, picking on the kind soul that gave you a ride so that your sorry ass wouldn't have to walk home. Not nice Harvey, not nice. Do you forget that I'm sweet as sugar?" I laughed then faked sadness with a pouty lip and puppy eyes. With a slow smile he said, "No Dyl, I could never forget anything about you. Not even quite sure you'd let me. Dyl, you always leave your impression." Confused and flattered, but trying to keep my attention on the road. We did not need another accident. When he asked, "What're ya thinking about?" Lying slightly, "Oh, the other night when I almost injured you with my watermelon sized head." Replying quickly he said, "Your head is just perfect Dyl. You're just perfect." At that comment, my stomach was a flutter. I had tingling between my legs and my whole body felt like it was on fire. I wanted to pull over the car, straddle his lap and crush my mouth to his so passionately that I spoiled him for all other women. But reality had a way of sinking in. I began to think of Max and what it would do to her if I did something so selfish. I adored my goofy friend, I couldn't hurt her in that way. She loved me and her brother, but no doubt she would've always chose him first, as it should've been. So attempting to curb my panic-stricken brain I blurted out, "So, umm you and Max umm were getting along really well tonight. Do you like her?" He seemed kind of stunned at my question and quickly replied, "Yeah, Max is a great girl and we have fun together, but I'm not ready for a relationship right now. That was why I needed to clear my head. I'm not quite over this other girl I've had a thing for. She's not interested." My heart dropped into my stomach swallowed it whole and crapped it out all at once. How could someone not possibly want this man? Holy hell, look at him! He was a total sex God! Who was this crazy hoe? As if he noticed my expression, he looked shocked and rushed to say, "Now Dyl look, it's okay I don't expect....."

I interrupted, "Well it's her fucking loss, you are amazing Jace! Fun, charming, sexy as hell. Shit if I didn't have a boyfriend right now, I'd throw you over the backseat and have my way with you." As I stopped at the light and finished those words I saw those blue eyes begin to darken, his chest began to rise and fall rapidly. He clenched and unclenched his hands repeatedly. Then suddenly stopped. He held his breath and I held mine. He leaned toward me and I toward him, until I could feel his breath on my lips, then he paused for just a moment before his lips grazed mine. It felt like he was trying to trace my lips with his, his breath felt so warm. He smelled like spearmint and something sweet. Did I mention I had a serious sweet tooth? He began to add more pressure and I felt the full force of what he was trying to tell me through this kiss. All I could think of right now was how I wanted his hands all over me. He reached out and started caressing my face with one hand as he ran his other hand through my hair. Oh, I'd dreamt of these hands on me. As, I began letting my hands roam up his firm chest, then down his strong arms to where his hands met mine and our fingers intertwined. His hands were so strong and so perfect. They fit mine perfectly, it was almost like they were made for me. I was lost in the moment until a loud horn pulled us out of our kiss. Our first real amazing, sensual and…….

totally wrong! Crazy! Holy fucking shit what did I just do? The light had turned green and the impatient driver behind us must've not wanted to go around, but I waved him around anyway. When I looked up at Jace, I could feel him analyzing this. Shit, what was I thinking? Talking like that to a guy would most definitely send the wrong signals. Not only was he messed up over some girl, I inadvertently hit on him on the drive home. Oh and poor Max, she could never find out. She'd hate me. I even think Nick would forgive me before she would. I needed her, she could never know. Then Jace spoke, "So, I guess that means that she may actually have a thing for me too?" He looked so vulnerable and hopeful. Holy Hell IT IS ME?! It wasn't like I had self-esteem issues, I liked myself. I even thought that I was pretty, but he knew I was spoken for. That was different than not being interested. I felt the blush, the heat, and the tingles, but I had to fight it. I couldn't lose her and Nick was a great guy. I could've done a lot worse than Nick. He was wonderful, but now I realized that I didn't deserve wonderful or even this amazing man in

A Minor Happy Ending

front of me. Jace looked fearful when I stared at him with sad and scared eyes, "Oh God Jace, this shouldn't have happened. I'm with Nick. Max is my best friend and I think she may like you. What am I supposed to say to them? Sorry, but I decided to be selfish and do whatever I pleased regardless of anybody's feelings." I immediately began to cry feeling guilty for both betraying my boyfriend and making Jace feel bad. What else could I had possibly screwed up now. As I cried, Jace leaned over and put the car in park. He pulled me over into his lap and I allowed it. In my ear he whispered , "Don't worry Dyl, I won't tell. You won't lose her. I know she's important to you." Not once did either of us show any concern for Nick and that just made me feel worse.

Chapter 8

      I was the worst friend in the world. How could have I betrayed her trust? She trusted me with her brother's heart and I just shit on it. Needless to say when I finally stopped sobbing and pitying myself, I took Jace home. He didn't want to go to Cam's tonight. The whole way there he was quiet and just kept his hand on the back of my neck, drawing circles with his calloused fingers in an attempt to sooth me. Oh, how I wanted his hands on me touching me. When he touched me it felt different than when Nick did. Nick was comfortable, but Jace was exciting. It was sensual. Like that was what his hands were made to do. Although, I loved every touch of his hands, I was relieved when we arrived at his home. I didn't need to be tempted anymore, obviously I couldn't control myself.

As Jace opened the passenger side door, he turned to look at me and said, "I won't tell, but I'm not quitting you either, Dyl. I know you want this too. I can feel it. I care enough about you to give you time to make up your mind.

A Minor Happy Ending

Max is your friend, she'll understand. I will wait, but I know what I want and it's you, . Only you." After he said his peace, he exited the car, as he slowly made his way to his front door hanging his head and pushing his hands deep into his pockets. He turned and said, "Dyl?" I nodded in his direction to acknowledge him. "You really do taste as sweet as sugar." Then that crooked grin appeared as he turned and sauntered into his house.

I couldn't get that grin or those lips out of my head the whole drive home. Those sweet, soft, and tasty lips. That man could kiss. That kiss would haunt every dream I'd ever have for my entire existence.

When I returned home, I snuck in the house not to wake my mom and sister. Mom usually slept soundly and was hard to rouse, but my sister could hear a pin drop. My sister Jenna was thirteen years old and thought she knew everything. She was the ultimate student, cheerleader, and softball player extraordinaire. She was busy for a teen, but she loved it. Mom kept her busy with activities since she was a single mother and wanted to make sure she stayed out of trouble. My mom was a nurse. She worked at a doctor's office 5 days a week and had been there for as long as I could remember. She started there as a receptionist, then received her nursing degree after our dad left us seven years ago. Jenna barely remembered him, but I remembered enough. All the fighting and complaining that mom was never doing enough even though she worked all the time. While his lazy ass only worked when the weather was good. Dad was a construction worker and never supplemented his income, leaving the majority of the responsibility to mom. We were better off in my opinion. All he did was tell us how worthless we were with a bottle of beer in his hand and a cigarette in the other. I realized he was the worthless one, around age ten, when I watched as my mom just got home from a 50 hour work week, sick as hell and he asked her when dinner would be ready after a long day of sitting on his ass. Then, when she refused he began to berate her in front of me. Watching this made me vow to never let a man, even my father have that control over me. No control at all. Needless to say, after he left, we made our new normal. A peaceful normal where mom, Jenna, and I lived. We were a team.

As I snuck in I was surprised to see my mother sitting at the kitchen table with a coffee and her book. "Nice to finally see my girl. So, Nick and Max didn't brainwash you and turn you into a stepford wife after all, huh?" she said sarcastically. Mom was pretty liberal. She didn't have any delusions about my innocence. She just always felt the need to remind me of my manners. As I rolled my eyes and chuckled at her dry comment, I muttered, "Got the point mother, I will make my whereabouts known. Haven't you had any stallions over to pass the time, while I've been gone." With an eye roll that put mine to shame, mom said, "When do I have time for that? And Dyllan Madeline, why are you home so late? Don't you get off at two?" With a little apprehension, I muttered, "Yeah, I gave a friend a ride home. Nick wanted me to sleep there tonight, but I have some laundry and other things to catch up on." Mom looked at me like she knew something and said. "Dyllan, is Nick treating you ok? Is there trouble in paradise?" How did she always know? That mothers intuition shit, I bet. My mom was so intuitive and I told her almost everything. So instead of insulting her with a series of lies she would read through, I just broke down and told her the events of the past few days. She seemed shocked about Nick professing his love, more shocked when I told her about the kiss. She listened for what seemed like hours and said not a word until I could no longer speak. I finished my story and hugged her good night. As I went to leave the room to get ready for bed, my mom said, "Dyllan, just remember that you just graduated high school and you don't have to be sure of everything yet. This is your time to explore the world. Have fun until you start college this fall. You don't need to figure out your life yet, you're young, enjoy it!" I decided that was a good way to end a crazy night with sound advice from my mom. "Good night momma, love you." She smiled and said, "You too baby girl."

Shaan Ranae

After I showered to wash away the grime from this day, I curled up in my bed and drifted off immediately to vivid dreams of dark blue eyes, sweet plump lips, and roaming calloused hands.

Chapter 9

When I awoke, I checked my phone for the time and saw that it was noon. I had four texts.

Nick: *Ok babe, I get it. It's fine. I'll call you tonight.*

Max: *Missed ya last night. Call me later. Needing some major BFF time.*

Jace: *Good morning Sugar, just checking on my FRIEND.*

Max: *Did you fall off the planet? WTH? Did you lose your phone again? Call me.*

There she was, my BFF. Ignoring the other two texts for the moment, I texted Max back.

Me: *What up Maxwell? Just woke up. Got to bed late.*

Max: *Well get your ass moving and pick me up. We are wasting the day away.*

Me: *Sorry but have laundry and some major resting to catch up on before work tonight since that brother of yours kept me busy all week.*

Max: *OOOOOkay. How about you pick me up and bring me to your house and we will hang out and do laundry and watch old movies*

She always knew how to get her way with me. I loved old movies. Something about them was magical to me.

Me: *All right brat, be ready I'm not changing out of my PJ's for anyone until work.*

Max: *Ill be ready!*

Me: *See you in 10.*

I picked Max up and it was like old times. Before Nick and Jace, all the drama that followed, but the guilt was killing me. Not only because of betraying Nick, but also guilty because what if she really liked Jace? So, I figured I would test the waters as we swooned over how the dancer glided across the floor sweeping up his partner into his arms and giving her a chaste kiss. "Awe, isn't he amazing, back when chivalry and manners were part of the courtship instead of – hey babe put your number in my phone and Ill text ya in between Xbox games with my boys." She chuckled at my comment and added one of her own, "Or they send so

A Minor Happy Ending

many mixed signals, you're not sure what they want." Hmmmm? I prepared myself for her to answer the question I was about to ask, so that I was not totally blind sided when she gave the answer that I wasn't sure that I wanted. "Who are we talking about here, girly? Anyone I know?" Bracing myself for her answer, she took a minute to respond. "Well, I'm not sure. There is this one guy, I guess. He's totally sweet. Man, he's so hot, but I'm not sure what he thinks about me. One day he's cuddling next to me whispering in my ear and the next day he seems like he doesn't notice that I'm in the room. And don't take this the wrong way, but I get a little jealous when he's around you. You are always so confident. . I know you aren't trying to steal my thunder, but when you're there, I don't feel like I'm even in the room." I quickly replied, "Awe baby girl, any man who doesn't see how special you are, isn't worthy of your awesomeness!" She chuckled at my over the top but totally true compliment. I continued on, "Now who is this totally hot guy? Maybe I can help." She quickly replied, "Not yet Dyl, I want to keep him to myself just for a little while. The only thing I'll say is that we hang out with him often." Well, that settled it. I could never be with Jace. Who else could she be talking about? I saw them cuddling together at The Diner. They've smoked weed together on many occasions and I had noticed the way she acted when he was paying attention to me. What did I do?

As I was mentally beating myself down, my phone chirped making me aware of a text message.

Jace: *I'm sorry Sugar. Am I not supposed to text you now? I didn't get the memo. Keep me posted.*

Really, ass! What happened to I'll wait? I won't tell. The voice in my head reminded me. WTF? So, out of a fit of anger and guilt as I stared at Max while I texted him back testing the waters.

Me: *Girls day ASS! Sorry, I'm not at your beck and call but I'm sure there are plenty of women who would literally bend over backwards to please you. I'm not a people pleaser. People please me.*

Jace: *Only if Sugar, Only if.*

I was speechless. That was what I got for texting before I thought. Now I couldn't get the vision of his calloused hands roaming my body beginning near my knee, slowly gaining momentum as they glided up my thighs to the warm moist area between my legs. As another chirp brought me out of my daydream, I saw

Jace: *Just worried about you Sugar, sorry to offend. Hope to see you soon.*

A Minor Happy Ending

Now I felt like an ass. A huge cellulite ridden ass! And why did he keep calling me sugar? I felt like I was in a bad eighties sitcom.

Me: *One last thing?*

Jace: *What's that?*

Me: *Sugar?*

Jace: *That's how you taste. As sweet as sugar. I'm curious how sweet you taste other places.*

Holy fuck me sideways!

Me: *Ok gotta go. Night.*

Jace: *Night.*

Holy hell this had to stop. How would I ever explain this? I couldn't help myself. He even seemed to enjoy my smart ass remarks. Nick would either give me a kind reprimand or blamed it on my age. Sometimes I thought that was our problem. Nick was too old for his age and I was not mature enough for mine. What did this prove? Nothing. I deleted the inappropriate messages, but the whole scene was imprinted in my head.

Chapter 10

    Max and I continued our movie marathon and laundry until I had to get ready for work. On my way to work, I dropped Max off at Cam's where I found my favorite group of crazies sitting on the porch listening to someone play the guitar. I stepped out of the car just to curb my curiosity over who was playing, I was totally stunned to see that it was Jace. He was playing the guitar and singing in hushed low tones on Cam's porch.

Really!? Now he had the whole sexy musician thing going on? God, this was not fair! Next thing I would've found out was that he rescued baby seals from oil spills in his free time and gave so much blood that there was no longer a shortage for his type.

He was amazing. Not a note or a lyric out of place and he seemed so comfortable singing in front of everyone. His voice was low and raspy like he was whispering to you. He was singing the rock ballad, that I was singing in the car. Was this for me? He sang the whole song with his eyes

A Minor Happy Ending

closed, but I could tell he knew I was there. I could feel it, when the song ended, he opened his eyes and that lazy grin began to surface. I felt a blush through my entire body and heat flooded into my lower belly. He could see it and he knew. "What made you start playing again, Jace?" Cam asked, bringing me out of my daze. He replied with a gleam in his eyes, "Let's just say I have a very sweet reason. It's totally worth it!" Then his eyes found mine as he held his guitar. I was jealous of the guitar. I felt like that was where I should be, in his arms, but... Shit, I've got to get to work. I made a quick recovery, "Night ya'll. Heading to work, those pancakes won't deliver themselves." I nodded and waved to everyone, they all yelled their goodbyes. The whole drive over, I kept hearing his voice wishing that I could've stayed and listened. Just having that and that alone to cherish him was enough. When I pulled into the parking lot of The Diner, a familiar car sat there and the owner jumped out when I arrived. Nick. I got out of the Century and made my way toward him a little guilt-stricken and a little surprised. I strolled up to him and he had a somber yet sincere look on his face. "Hi, sweet girl," he whispered as I wrapped my arms around his waist and rested my head on his chest. After I breathed in all things Nick and sighed, I found and stayed in the comfort that those arms had been giving me lately. I felt safe. After my anxiety subsided I answered honestly, "I've missed these arms." I thought I heard a sigh and felt him relax. He kept rubbing his hands up and down my back in soothing motions. Then he spoke, "Babe, what happened last night? I was afraid something happened to you. Then I saw your message and listened to your voicemail. Then I figured that I'd give you some space since I dropped a bomb on you the other night. I'm not sorry, though. I do love you babe. I understand you're young, shit so am I! I only have two years on you. You've just become my everything and I don't want to lose you. I just want you to know there is no pressure about us babe. No proposals coming or grand gestures, just you knowing I love you is enough for me." While he continued to hold me in his arms and caressed me to an almost comatose state. I kept thinking how stupid I was, the guilt over took me and I blurted, "Last night I took Jace home and we kissed. It was a mistake. It was so stupid Nick. So stupid!" His whole body tensed and he just let me go. The look on his face was unreadable except for maybe a slight look of disgust. All he had was Max and me. Of course, I just had to fuck it all up. Without a word he got in his car and drove away. Stupid girl.

A Minor Happy Ending

Chapter 11

I worked my shift and headed home to sulk in private. Awaiting the calls and texts from my friends telling me what a douche bag I was for hurting not only Nick but Max too. Nothing came. Silence. So, I guess this was how it was supposed to have been. I drifted off into sleep not remembering what I dreamed of or even if I dreamt at all. I slept way into the next day.

I still haven't heard a word from anyone by 5 p.m. that night, my cell hadn't chirped all day. I couldn't even bring myself to check it, in case Max had left nasty texts for being a whore who not only broke her brother's heart, but hers. Nothing.

Thinking I'd rather be screamed at! As I sat in my room sulking and totally feeling sorry for myself, I gathered enough courage to text Max and maybe get the verbal lashing I'd been expecting all day. I grabbed my phone off of the coffee table and realized it'd been off all day. I plugged in my phone, powered it up to find 14 unanswered texts. Some from Max, Jade, and Jace, but nothing from Nick. Taking a deep breath, I opened my first text from Max.

Max: *Hey what's up with Nick? He's grouchy and you're not here. Everything ok?*

20 minutes later.

Max: *Dyl, did you guys fight? Was he mean to you? Please, I'm worried about you?*

Two more followed last night with the same worried tone to them. She didn't know. Why hadn't Nick told her what a terrible person I was? The next text I saw was from Jace.

Jace: *Just spoke with Max. She said she couldn't get a hold of you. Are you ok, Dyl?*

A little while later

Jace: *You need to just let me know if you are ok, Dyl.*

After that just random texts from Jade telling me some off the wall shit, she knew that I'd normally love to hear. I sat on the couch contemplating if I should text Max and test the waters, but fear won and I texted Jace instead.

Me: *I'm alive and safe. My phone was off and I was sleeping. I do work late, ya know. Sorry I'm a bother.*

He replied within seconds

Jace: *You're never a bother to me Sugar. I'm glad you're safe. Max was worried so I was too. So, what happened to*

A Minor Happy Ending

make Max worry so much. She called everyone looking for you.

I wasn't sure what to say to him. I haven't even spoken with Nick or Max about all of this, but I needed to speak to someone.

Me: *I'll call ya*

Jace: *Better yet, come and pick me up.*

Against my better judgment, I agreed. After I showered and put on clean clothes, I headed over to Jace's to talk. He lived on the wealthier side of town, but you'd never guess by looking at him. He dressed casually, like a regular guy. As I pulled into the driveway, I saw his front door open and he came sauntering out with his lazy walk like he didn't have a care in the world. As he approached the Century, his crooked smile was displayed on his lips and was the sexiest thing I'd ever seen. Pretty much everything about this man was the sexiest thing I'd ever seen. He opened up the passenger side door, slid in and without thinking, I leaned over and gave him a lingering hug and a soft whisper-like kiss to his neck. The heat that generated between us was so strong, I felt my insides on fire. He pulled back, stared into my wanting eyes and said, "Not now Dyl, Not until you are mine." I leaned back, took a deep breath to relax myself as he took a hold of my hand. I looked at him with exhaustion, he said, "Friends can hold hands, I can't not touch you Dyl. When I'm around you, I can't stop myself okay." I accepted this statement as a truth and left our fingers intertwined, while he rubbed small circles on the back of my hand. I knew this probably wasn't the smartest thing for me to do right now with all of this Nick confusion going on, but this small gesture made me feel treasured and safe.

We drove to a park a couple of towns over to avoid anyone we knew. I parked the Century, we exited leisurely walking through the park and finding our fingers intertwined again. This time it felt more natural. Nothing was forced with Jace, it always felt easy. Our conversations, even about the dumbest things, seemed to flow freely.

While strolling through the park, we came upon this older couple sitting on a bench. They were holding hands and talking like two teenagers in love. I watched them as they cuddled and laughed together. It brought a smile to my face as I turned to see his dark blue eyes staring at me with sincerity and something else that I couldn't describe. As his crooked smile made an appearance, I felt mine grow as well. Then he shrugged his shoulders and pulled me along. "That's the dream", I heard him say. I shrugged noncommittally. He continued "Well, don't you think it would be cool to find someone and be with them for the next fifty years? I find it amazing that he's watched her slowly grow old. Watched her belly grow with his babies

and watched her when she discovered her first gray hair. Do you see how he looks at her? You would never be able to tell that she had any flaws by looking through his eyes. Someone to spend your life with and loves you every day. She stays through it all, when you're grouchy or you're just a little bit fat. She always looks at you like you are the most precious thing in her world. That's the dream Dyl."
I wasn't quite sure what to say at that point. With my cheeks blushing, I provided him with a shy smile and a nod. It was like he knew what to say. That was why I loved those old movies. They reminded me of a time when it was meant to be forever. Sometimes I felt like I came from another time.

"Sometimes I feel like an old soul, sorry Sugar, didn't mean to drag you down." Jace said bringing me out of my own head. De ja vu weird! I looked up into his eyes and fixed my gaze. I didn't want to look anywhere else or talk with anyone else. I just wanted to be here with his hand in mine for the next fifty years. These last few hours felt like minutes, so what's another fifty years or so? Maybe he wouldn't mind. I couldn't bring my gaze from his while he took his other hand and brushed my strawberry blonde hair from my face. Man, I loved the feel of his calloused hands touching me. Anywhere they touched me was amazing. I could spend the rest of my days with his calloused fingers touching me. The pull between us grew stronger, when I was just about to give into temptation and fall, he abruptly twirled me away from him. I had to say that I was a little relieved at the gesture. He was twirling me like the dancers in the movies, it took the tension out of the moment. Then he brought me back to him until I felt his hard body so close to mine swaying with the imaginary music playing in our minds. He threw in random odd dancing moves to make me laugh. He seemed to enjoy making me laugh. His eyes lit up every time. Then the last time he twirled me, we just stopped and breathed each other in, staring into each other's eyes. He leaned in, I smelled the mint on his breath, felt the warmth from his lips. I wanted those lips on me, but I wasn't ready. I couldn't seem to pull myself away. I felt like I couldn't take anymore of his stare and of his hands on me, when he backed away keeping my grasp, walking away from the sweet couple. "Not until you're mine." I heard him say.

    We found a small fountain near the back of the park and sat there with our hands still clasped together. I was enjoying our quiet time, when Jace finally asked, "Now, what has you so upset that Max nor anyone else could find you? Why wouldn't you answer your phone or texts?" I replied shortly, "It's not like I disappeared, I was at home and accidentally shut my phone off." He replied," Okay?" then after a long drawn out silence I replied , "Nick

A Minor Happy Ending

was acting strange and I wasn't there, so she thought something was wrong." Sounding stressed, I tried to act as if it were nothing, but he could see right through me. "Dyl, listen we're still friends. You can tell me. I may not enjoy it, but I'll listen." I looked up into his sincere eyes and melted. I knew he cared, I could tell him anything. That was when the flood gates burst. I told him how I confessed to Nick about the kiss and he just left me. At the mention of Nick's name, his whole body tensed up, but I pretended not to notice. I kept trying to explain my feelings for Nick as well as my feelings toward him, but not once did he steer a judgmental look in my direction. Not once. He just listened with concern etched across his face and a firm grip on my hand. After all the tears dried, all the tension was finally gone, from what seemed like hours of venting. I looked up to find him looking defeated. I felt terrible confessing all of my feelings and causing him sadness. To ease his mind I said, "Bet I don't look like such a prize right now, probably more like the bride of frankenstein." He just looked at me with a sad smile and said, "Always the most beautiful girl around." Then he stood and continued, letting go of my hand, "I think we should head back, it sounds like you have some things to think about and a friend to talk to." He was right, but suddenly the only thing I was worried about was that his hand was no longer in mine. I missed his warm touch. We walked back to the car in silence. Not hand in hand this time, but together nonetheless. We slid into the Century and made our way towards home. As I parked in his drive way, he turned to me and said, "I'm giving you all the time you need because I know this is supposed to be Dyl, but I see how hard this is for you and I can't watch you suffer. Make your decision. Tell Max. I'll be happy with whatever you choose, but I can't watch you be miserable because of me." Then he quickly hopped out of the car without another word and walked into his house.

Taking the long way home, I sulked and contemplated how I was going to break it to Max that I hurt her brother. Also, how was I going to tell her I had feelings for the same guy she did?

A Minor Happy Ending

Chapter 12

As I pulled into my driveway, a familiar car sat with Nick sitting in it looking sad and anxious. When I got out of my car, he was standing so close to me that I wasn't sure I could breathe. Before I could speak, he rushed to say, "Baby, I'm so sorry . You were honest and I shut you out. Please forgive me?"

REALLY! WTF? ARE YOU SERIOUS?   He was apologizing to me! It was like I'd stepped into the twilight zone. I was the bad guy here. I was the one that should be sorry. I looked up at him confused and asked, "Why are you here, Nick?" sounding sad. He quickly replied, "Babe, didn't you hear me? I'm sorry. I shouldn't have left. I should've let you explain. Max told me that you were missing. I was worried that something happened to you." He grabbed me and held me the way that used to make me tingle all over, but now all I felt was comfort. I had comfort that nothing was broken and that Max didn't hate me.

Also, I was relieved that he didn't hate me; not having Nick around would be terrible. He was one of my best friends, but I wasn't feeling the butterflies anymore. I looked up into Nick's eyes hoping to find that there were still feelings there and we could just go back. When I did all I felt was the companionship of a dear friend. He leaned down to kiss me and I let him, hoping to feel a spark of something there. Nothing. Something that used to cause electricity to run through my veins couldn't even keep my attention. My mind wandered to the kiss I shared with Jace. A kiss no other kiss could compare to. It would just be easier if I could love Nick back. When I opened my eyes, love was not what I felt. I looked hesitantly in his direction, his return gaze showed me his understanding. "You don't want me at all, do you? Not even after all this time?" I could see the light in his eyes dim, I began to panic and muttered, "No, I just need time. I'm confused and exhausted after these last few days. I'm not sure what I want." I lied, but I thought I meant it at the time. "So, what does this mean?" he growled in frustration. "I don't know Nick" I answered honestly not wanting to make this any worse. He grabbed me by the arms and crushed me to him again. He was holding onto me as if I was going to disappear, I wasn't so sure I wouldn't . I stayed there to comfort him for a while, but then placed a kiss to his cheek and told him goodbye. With a sad smile he let me go and

A Minor Happy Ending

said, "I'll wait as long as I have to, you are it for me. I won't say good bye." Then I watched as he strode to his car. My heart broke for that sweet man who wished to wait for me. As a matter of fact, I had two sweet men waiting for me, I wasn't sure that I deserved either one. As my first tear fell, I stood on my porch watching as Nick left until I no longer could see his car, that was when the damn broke and I became a sobbing mess. As I curled into myself on the front porch, a small touch on my shoulder brought me out of my fog. "C'mon baby girl, let's go in." my mom said tenderly.

Mom took me inside, handed me a cup of black coffee as I began to spill everything that happened. She was always so amazing and listened without judgment. She advised me to take a break from both men and decide if I even wanted someone right now. I thought that sounded like the best advice I've received yet. Time for a break from dating and just being me again.

Chapter 13

It was finally time to bite the bullet and call Max if she'd even answer. So, I sat on the corner of my bed and took a deep breath, slowly exhaling every bit of my nervous energy from my body. I scanned through the names on my phone and pressed send. It rang twice and I heard "It's about time, you crazy hoe! I've been texting you forever. You had me worried sick!" After her crazy rant, I finally spoke, "So, we're okay?" sounding sheepish. "Look, I know something is up with you and Nick and that's between you two, but If you ever disappear on me again, there will be major consequences. Got it ?" With relief I replied, "Got it, babes." She quickly replied, "Now come pick my ass up and we can meet Jade and Cam at The Diner." "Sounds good, I'll get ready and be there in thirty, okay?" I asked. "It's a plan. See you soon." My mood was lifted a little and I was actually excited over something without guilt clouding my thoughts. As I washed up, my mind wandered

A Minor Happy Ending

to Jace, thinking of our fingers intertwined, walking and talking as if we'd known each other forever. I kept thinking of his dream, so simple and easy like him. He kept sneaking in my thoughts, even though the only thing I wanted to think about was taking a break.

On the drive over to Max's I turned on the radio to hear one of my favorite songs. I turned the radio up as loud as I could and sang at the top of my lungs on the short drive. When I pulled in, I texted Max to let her know I had arrived. I didn't want to go inside and risk seeing Nick, knowing I would cave in and crawl back to him. I did care for him. I just didn't know how much. Their front door opened, Max came rushing out with Nick on her heels. I forced a tight smile and my whole body tensed. He stopped on the porch when he saw my reaction and just waved goodbye with a sad smile. I waved in return and prayed that I was doing the right thing. "C'mon bitch let's go!" she said. Oh, how I loved our little pet names for each other. "We need to pick up Jade and Cam, they're at Cam's house. Oh, and by the way, we are going dancing tonight." Dancing? What happened to The Diner? Confused, I commented, "I'm not dressed to go dancing." She gave me an exasperated look and said, Cam has something for you to borrow for tonight. We are going to dress you up, get you drunk, and flirt with cute guys. You still have your fake ID, right Wilma Picklesimer?" She said with a wicked smile that caused a mirrored reaction from me. "That's right Anita Holder." I replied as I remembered the day the two of us picked out the two most hilarious names that we could think of for our IDs.

We laughed and sang along with the music playing on the radio the entire way to Cam's. I felt carefree at the moment, but in the back of my mind I knew I had some issues to work on. For now, I decided it was time to blow off some steam.
We arrived at Cam's to find the girls sitting on the front porch smoking and laughing. We exited the car and greeted our girls. "What's up bitches?" Max and I said in unison. We were greeted with smiles and hugs. After some small talk, Cam said, "Well girls, let's go get ready to break some hearts tonight!" I cringed at her words, Jade came to the rescue as usual, "Smooth Cam, I think you need some meds girl, diarrhea of the mouth is a serious condition. You should probably have that looked at." As she linked her arm with mine and pulled me through the door.

We spent the next couple of hours primping, now I had to pick out something to wear. Cam and I were close to the same size, except I was a little fuller in the chest. She was also about 4 inches taller than me too. So, pants were out of the question. I didn't usually wear dresses, but my

A Minor Happy Ending

choices were limited. Max appeared from behind me with a dress dangling from her fingers and said, "Ya can't go wrong with a little black dress and I have these black strappy heels to match." Oh man, the last time I wore heels was at my cousins wedding, I almost twisted my ankle three times. Now, this time I would be drunk in heels while wearing a dress. As if Max could read my mind she spoke up, "You'll be fine. You've been way less clutzy lately." I rolled my eyes and gave her my 'oh puleez' face. Then I went into the bathroom and put on the dress. Huh, not half bad. Who knew I would look like that in a dress. I doubt I had proper dress etiquette memorized. Thank God I wore lace underwear, otherwise I'd have to go commando under this thing. The nice thing about the little black dress was that it also looked good with my skin. I didn't tan well, but I wasn't pale either. My legs looked good with their muscular build from all of my waitressing. The dress was a little snug in the chest, but unless I duct taped the girls down, I was just going to have to improvise ways to keep them under control. After I slipped into the heels, the whole package was complete, I had to say that I liked this look. I felt beautiful and confident. I'd always been comfortable in my appearance, but wearing dresses was foreign. After I touched up my lip gloss, we all stood together in the mirror and heard Jade asked, "Guess who is getting drunk for free tonight?" the rest of us just began to giggle. We headed out to the car, just as we were getting in Jade pulled me aside and said, "It'll be fine. Just do it right and she'll be fine. I know you will. Now let's go and deal with tomorrow, tomorrow!" Her clairvoyance was creepy sometimes!

The four of us climbed into the Century, dressed and ready for a girls night out when I asked, "Now, where to ladies?" Cam looked at me incredulously and stated, "Well Club 43 of course" attempting to sound upper class snooty. I smiled at her attempt and concurred, "Well of course." The ride didn't take long when we ended up at Club 43. Club 43 was usually populated with college students as well as an occasional creeper who was attempting to relive some of their youth during their mid-life crisis. We went to dance. We entered and the atmosphere tonight was thick with sweat and sex. There were bodies rubbing against one another, the music was loud and I could feel the beat pulse through my limbs. It was just what I was looking for. I could dance with an anonymous stranger, get drunk, and have fun with my girls. But first things first, "Who is DD?" Max was quick to answer, "I've got that covered. Don't worry." she claimed with a knowing smile. "Okay, cool" I said knowing that she wouldn't purposely put me in a bad situation. We made it up to the bar and ordered our first drinks for tonight. We sipped on those and people watched. As we observed the

A Minor Happy Ending

different people entering the club and dancing with each other, we made up stories about their lives. The person with the best story won a free drink from the challenger. Jade and I started this game one slow night at The Diner ages ago. Tonight Jade and I found a little blonde in a baby doll dress sipping her drink seductively through a straw and giving this guy in a polo shirt the 'fuck me' eyes. He noticed and stuck his chest out a little more while smiling at her. Jade made up an amazingly funny story that she was actually an undercover agent destined to take down an illegal sex toy ring. Our gentleman friend here, was the ring leader for a blow-up doll chain that was causing an epidemic of penis burn throughout the entire midwest. That almost won the drink, but I thought up a story really quick. "I'm not so sure Jade, she does strike me as the secret agent type, but I was thinking more along the lines of serial killer. Do you see how she keeps applying that lip gloss? I have a feeling that's how she draws them in, with promises of great blow jobs and a night nestled between her twins. She lures them back to her hotel room, castrates them and suffocates them with their own penises. That lip gloss she has is a numbing agent and the guy doesn't even realize it until it's too late. When they open their mouth in shock, she shoves it in. Blow job Betty strikes again," I finished with a smile on my face. At the same time, the guy approached 'Betty' as she began to lick her straw with a little more zest and our table erupted in laughter. Max declared it a tie and we had to buy our own next round.

Before I grabbed my next drink Max and I decided that we wanted to dance. We left Cam and Jade to flirt with these two semi-sexy guys that just sat at the table next to us. Max and I made it out onto the dance floor and began to move. Max could dance. She was amazing, I was always worried about someone taking it too far, misconstruing her amazing dance skills as hitting on them. She looked like a vixen on the dance floor, but she was innocent. I could dance, but I paled in comparison to Max. As we got lost in the music, I swore I saw Smith come up behind Max and roam his hands all over her. She didn't seem to mind, plus it was Smith. Then I felt someone come up from behind me. Hello, Mr. Anonymous. I'd been waiting for you. I could turn to see who this was, but nah! I was up for some fun. No names, No faces. As he rubbed his body against me from behind, I felt a rush of heat through my body and between my legs. He began to rub his hands up the length of my sides and it felt amazing. I continued to move my pelvis grinding up against his length, feeling him harden with my gesture. I could smell him now. He smelled familiar, good familiar.

Max and Smith disappeared in the bodies on the dance floor, as I was dragged backwards a ways and thrusted up against a wall. My eyes searched for help, but then I looked up to see those beautiful blue eyes staring into mine. His chest was heaving. His body was rock hard everywhere and I loved the feel of it pressed up against me. We danced like this for numerous songs. I found myself increasingly warm and without thinking, without caring at this moment in time, I slipped my fingers into his short hair. I tugged just enough to cause a small growl to escape from his perfect lips and began to grind myself against him. My breathing had increased causing my chest to rise and fall rapidly. Right as our lips began to touch, I felt his strong hands grasp my hips and hold me against his length. He breathed, "You are mine, Dyl!" and at that moment I knew it. I was his. No one had ever made me react this way. That's when I felt his lips land on mine. At first he pressed hard, but then lighter grazes, small tastes with his tongue. Then his hands began to roam down my sides and around my hips landing on my ass. He grabbed me and pulled me closer. He broke the kiss long enough to whisper "Dyl you are killing me in this dress. I want to mame any man that looks at you and Sugar they are looking. The thought of another man touching this" as he caressed my ass through my dress, "or these" as his hands roamed to my breasts, he caressed my nipples through my dress. Then left his one hand on my breast and let the other roam between my legs "and definitely not this, Dyl. This is mine." I was drenched. I could feel the wetness between my legs and the blush began to crawl up my neck and into my cheeks. "Sugar, never be shy over what I do to you. I love that I drench these. I love that I cause that reaction in you. I need to touch you" he said as his fingers slipped into the lace, I felt the lace being torn away from my body causing me to flood yet again . "You're so wet for me Sugar." I felt his fingers enter my folds, I gasped at his touch. Then his finger entered me, filling me and causing my whole body to tighten instantly. He continued to thrust his finger into my warmth until I was panting against his lips. He pressed his body closer to mine and whispered, "Let go Dyl." And I did. I felt the world and all it's worries fall away with him this close, filling me with his fingers and causing my release with just a few words. Just when I felt the moan leave my lips, he covered my mouth with his absorbing my sounds and causing my climax to linger. When I came down from my high, I looked up into his beautiful blue eyes and felt home. He confirmed in this moment that I was his.

He brought me out of my daze saying, "Say it Dyl, I need to hear you say you're mine." No matter what happened after this point I could no longer lie to myself or anyone else, I was his. "I'm yours" I whispered against his lips then I roughly added pressure to those beautiful lips. As my hands roamed up his chest to the neckline of his shirt and

A Minor Happy Ending

grasped it roughly inhaling his scent, tasting his mouth, nipping and sucking on his lips and tongue. When we broke the kiss, I was staring into his eyes when we heard someone clear their throat.

Both of us stunned by the noise, we turned to see Cam standing there with a smirk on her face. "Hey, we're going to head out? Max had a few too many shots. Smith is going to drive us back to my place. Do you think that you can get Dyllan home? Max and Jade are crashing at my place, Dyl you are welcome too." She asked, but I was sure she knew the answer. When Jace spoke up for us both, "No thanks Cam we have things to discuss and Dyl needs to rest for tomorrow." Cam nodded and gave Jace a caring smile that only a good friend could give, so I felt our secret was safe for now. But I couldn't help but wonder, tomorrow? What was happening tomorrow? I looked at him out of the corner of my eye, that crooked grin I loved had returned, he grabbed my hands and walked us back onto the dance floor when he whispered, "But I get a few more dances with you before we leave." And I was more than happy to comply.

About an hour later, we were getting into my car. He was driving my Century. He chuckled as he moved the seat back and made a remark about my short legs. As I feigned offense, he was quick to remark, "Sexy ass short legs that I can't wait to have wrapped around my body!" My mouth dropped open at his comment, when he added another, "If they'll reach?" That comment earned him an eye roll and a Hardy Har Har from me, but made me smile just the same. Our banter was easy. Just being around him was easy. He made me feel that he was grateful that I was in the same room.

Since I'd had a few drinks, I didn't pay attention to where Jace was taking me. I was more focused on watching those lips and the way his chest moved when he breathed. Wishing I was brave enough to rub my hand up and down his toned arms and legs, I rubbed circles on my legs instead. When he turned and looked my way, he gave me a knowing smile, intertwined our fingers and set our hands on his lap. Feeling much more relaxed, I looked up and noticed that we were on his side of town. It brought me out of my fog long enough to ask, "Where are we going?" He looked at me then focused on the road and said, "I'm not ready to be away from you yet. I'm bringing you home with me. Don't worry my parents aren't home. They're never there. They are out of town on business again. Mom's in Cozumel with her business partner, James and Dad and his secretary are in Fiji for a conference. Will you stay with me tonight, Dyl? Just sleep. When he was completely gone, we will re-evaluate, but right now I just want you here." Wow! That was a lot of information for a drunken mind, but I agreed because I didn't want to be away from him

A Minor Happy Ending

either. Just being around him lifted my heart.

"I just need to let my mom know I won't be home, I don't want her to worry." He nodded and smiled at me. I texted mom, let her know that I wouldn't be home and she texted back to be safe. I loved my mom. She didn't push any agenda. She just wanted me safe. Jace's voice gained my attention, "That's cool that you check in with her." "Yeah, she's amazing. She just wants to know that I'm okay." With a sad smile he said, "That's great Dyl, cherish it." As we pulled into his driveway, I looked up at this nice two story colonial style home. His parents must be well off.

My mom worked tons of hours for our small little Cape Cod style home, just big enough for us. "Is it just your parents and you? No brothers or sisters?" I asked seeing how lonely he looked as he peered at the house. After he took a deep breath, he replied, "No, just my parents and me. They are probably only here a couple of days every other week. My mom owns her own decorating firm and my dad is an executive for Wheeler and Jax advertising firm in the city and both of them travel most days. We make it a point to spend every other Sunday together for dinner." He didn't sound too happy about his Sunday dinners, but I decided to change the subject to help take away his sadness. As we exited the Century, I said "Wow, your house is beautiful. I bet you could fit my house in here three times." He shrugged as he walked up to the front door and we entered. The inside was just as beautiful as the outside. Tiled floors, white walls and tasteful furniture covered the first floor. I was almost afraid to walk in, fearing that I'd mess up the pristine look of the place. It had a sterile feel to it. This place didn't feel like a home and that was when I looked up to find Jace with an expression of embarrassment on his face. "What's wrong?" as I stroked his cheek with my hand, I tried to take away the sad look on his face. He replied, "Maybe we should go. I thought if I brought you here…" he paused then continued after a long sigh, "I thought since you always feel like home to me that you could make this place feel like a home too." My stomach dropped and I grabbed him. To reassure him, I ran my fingers through his hair and I told him that I felt at home with him too. We made it up to his room. His room was like him warm and inviting. Warm colors and of course with posters of classic rock bands hanging on the wall. I looked around in awe trying to learn a little more about Jace. When my eyes landed on the guitar in the corner of the room, I asked, "How long have you played the guitar, you were amazing the other night?" That crooked smile returned, he told me how he'd played since he was a child when his Uncle taught him. He played until about three years ago when his Uncle passed away and he hadn't played again until the other night at Cam's.

A Minor Happy Ending

He told me that the night he confesses feelings for me was what he called, his 'd-day'. He decided if I didn't show any interest in him when he told me how he felt that he would move on and let me be happy with Nick. He also told me that he could tell that I didn't care for Nick the same way that Nick did for me. That hurt a little. He said he finally gave in when he saw us together and knew that wasn't what I really wanted. He saw more heat within the looks that we gave each other and could tell it was forced on my part. That made me feel guilty. I shouldn't have dragged him along and I was going to have to completely break it off. Hopefully, Max won't hate me, but it's not fair to keep Nick in limbo waiting for me to make a decision when I've known all along what I've wanted.

In return, I explained to Jace my feelings for him. I was able to speak freely with him about what I feared. He listened and understood grabbing my hand for comfort, never taking his eyes off of mine. Sitting on his bed, pouring out my heart to him was easy. I wanted him to know everything about me, I didn't have any fear that he would judge me. We talked into the early morning hours until we were comfortable on his bed, with him holding me against his chest whispering in my ear. I couldn't make out everything he was saying, but feeling his breath on me was enough to relax me into sleep, where I dreamt of his arms around me.

Chapter 14

I awoke with strong arms wrapped around my waist and his scent surrounding me. I could breathe him in all day, but, unfortunately, I was human and I had to pee. As I attempted to release myself from his iron grip, his arms tightened and a smile flashed across his lips. He leaned down and pressed his lips to mine before saying with a gravelly voice, "Good morning Sugar, did you dream of me?" I smiled and nodded at his sweet gesture this morning. He made me feel that my presence alone made his day. Feeling a little shy I asked sheepishly, since I really needed to pee, "Can you let me up, please?" He grabbed me tighter and shook his head. "Sorry, but you're stuck with me all day! Right here in this bed." I wiggled trying to get loose and he began to tickle my ribs until I was convulsing. I finally yelled out "STOP!" He looked a bit panicked at my tone, well I guess I should put him out of his misery and spill the beans, "I have to pee" I muttered

A Minor Happy Ending

under my breath. Then he said something that I would never expect, "Just do it! It'll be warm." Eww!

When I looked at him, he winked and laughed, "Okay but make it quick!" Oh My God, I thought he was serious. The bathroom adjoined his room, I ran the water so he couldn't hear me pee and I could've sworn I heard him chuckle from the other room. As I realized that I had some serious morning breath, I asked through the door, "Do you have an extra toothbrush?" He yelled back through the door to check the medicine cabinet, which in my opinion gave me snooping rights. When I opened the medicine cabinet, I did find an extra toothbrush and an economy size box of condoms. Holy hell how experienced was he? I'd only been with a couple of guys, they weren't that experienced either. As I continued to keep snooping, there was a knock on the door, I heard his voice with a jovial intonation, "When you're done investigating. Come down stairs, I'm making breakfast." Shit how did he know.

Coming out of the bathroom, I realized I was still wearing that silly black dress from last night and I searched for something to put on. I found a pair of black shorts and a worn camp T-shirt and put them on. I descended the stairs engulfed in the aroma of what smelled like waffles and bacon frying. Mmmm, a man after my own heart, I loved meat! As I tiptoed into the kitchen to surprise him, the air thickened, he knew I was there. When he slowly turned to find me wearing his clothes, his eyes almost turned black. He visually molested me. A shiver slid down my spine. That crooked grin of his made an appearance, he shook his head, "Dyl, baby I like the way you look in my clothes. But if you keep staring at me like that I will not be able to control myself any longer", he placed his arms around my waist, placed his head in my neck and breathed in. "I like that you smell like me, too." He said with his sexy ass growl. Not sure if it was from just waking up or from the reaction of us, I smiled hoping it was the latter. I placed my hands on his chest and tapped it twice to push away the tension between us and said, " No matter how tempting you are, I have something to do before we can proceed any further." He turned off the stove and grabbed my hand with a rush toward the door, saying, "Let's go Dyl!" I abruptly stopped and stared at him like he'd grown two heads and muttered, "Not yet I'm not even dressed yet and you are not going. I have to do this on my own." A huge smile appeared on his lips and he said, "Okay, just checking on where we stand." He tricked me. Exhausted and frustrated I groaned loudly, he just smiled in return.

He finished making breakfast and we ate quietly.

After we finished, I decided that it was time for me to take care of our little situation. He made me promise to call him after my talk with Nick. He placed a small kiss to my lips,

A Minor Happy Ending

"that was a small taste and I can't wait to taste more when you're completely mine." I hurried to the Century and headed home.

Mom and Jenna were nowhere to be found, I was determined to get this day over with. I showered and went over to Max and Nick's. It was only nine thirty, Max should've still been asleep, that should've given Nick and I some privacy.

As I drove over there, I contemplated the things I was going to say. I didn't want to tell him that I never loved him, but I didn't. I still wanted to be his friend. I cared for him so much, but just not in the same way anymore. I pulled into the drive, Smith's car was there. I was wondering if he decided to stay with Max and Nick instead of making the long trek home. I walked toward the front door and checked for the spare key. I grabbed it and placed it into the door quietly, hoping not to wake anyone up. The living room was empty, so I went to peek in Max's room to find her wrapped up in Smith's arms sleeping comfortably. My heart leapt for her and to be completely honest a bit for myself too. Knowing that she liked Smith and not Jace actually made me half giddy. Now a nervous knot formed in my belly as I made my way to the other side of their home to speak with Nick. I knocked, but no answer. So, I quietly opened the door, feeling absolutely terrible about the way I was going to wake him up and ruin his day. I almost turned around, but I heard an unfamiliar noise. It sounded female. So out of pure curiosity, I opened the door wide to find Nick lying in bed with a naked brunette with her back to me, straddling his waist and moving seductively on his lap. They didn't hear me knock since they were too busy with each other, then the girl turned and stared at me with a devious little smile on her face. It was Cam. The hatred radiating off of her was enough to push me back a few steps causing me to knock into his dresser. Anger boiled up inside of me, the next thing I saw was Nick's recognition that I was there. "DYL?" I turned and closed the door, as I heard rustling around and shouting coming from the bedroom. "DYL!" the voice got louder as I feared he was beginning to chase me. I began to run and made it out the front door before my legs gave out from shock and exhaustion over this entire situation. I was on the ground. I sat at the foot of the porch on my knees when I felt him looming behind me.

 "Really… Cam!" I exclaimed waiting for an answer. I heard a loud rush of air as he exhaled roughly, and stated, "And where were you last night, Dyllan? " Shock must've masked my features since Nick had a knowing look on his face and fear in his eyes, "Well?" with a little louder tone. I just sat there as he went on, "Cam told me that you went home with him. That was the last straw for me. I would've waited, but she showed me a picture of the two of you at

A Minor Happy Ending

the club looking pretty cozy. I would've waited, but not while you're fucking him." I couldn't look him in the eyes, but in an attempt to defend myself, I shouted, "I didn't fuck him!" Then he grabbed me and lifted me to him. He stared into my eyes to see if I was lying. I saw it the moment that he realized that I was telling the truth. Realization hits, I saw the panic in his eyes, "Oh fuck! Baby this is so stupid. I'm so sorry. Why did I believe her? Fuck Dyl this is messed up! I just wanted to feel better. I was devastated." That was when my bravery kicked in and in a monotone voice I replied, "Nick, I'm not so innocent. I didn't fuck him, but I did more than I should've. I think this is it. We've just made this easier on ourselves. We have both fucked it up and it can't be fixed. Go find yourself a nice girl that can love you like you deserve. Cam isn't worth your time. You're too good for her and were always too good for me." He stared into my pained eyes, his began to water, he whispered "Dyl," then unexpectedly brushed his lips against mine. He encircled his arms around me with a short and tight squeeze. He pulled back to look at me, but I knew he could see that it was over, then turned and walked away. I could've sworn I heard him say I love you as he walked back into the house with his head hung low.

 Hopefully, Max won't wake to see Cam with her claws into Nick. YUCK, Cam! Fuck, what a friend she was. Surely that was her intention last night, her master plan to get me to go home with Jace, so she could try to fuck Nick. She always wanted what was mine. As I got into the Century, I allowed my mind to wander and the sadness overcame . Sadness for what Nick and I had, the friendship, the intimacy, and even the over protective quality he had when he was mine. No matter what I felt for Jace, I still felt a loss. Nick was a big part of my life, now that part was gone. I drove home to shower the pain away.

A Minor Happy Ending

Chapter 15

I pulled the Century into the driveway, turned off the engine and just sat. What a cluster fuck! I felt anguish over the way we ended. I wasn't jealous, but I felt betrayed. Cam stabbed me right in the back. If she would've asked me , she probably could've had my blessing, but to sneak behind my back. UGH, I was done with her. I could feel the hate and triumph rolling off of her in waves. She was getting off knowing it was with my boyfriend. This was just a big game for her. So, I wondered what this would mean for Jace and me. They'd been friends for years; they were practically brother and sister. Well, there was only one way to find out. I grabbed my cell and dialed Jace's number. It rang twice before he answered. "Hello Sugar, I wasn't expecting your call so soon. How'd it go? Are you doing okay?" That was when the damn broke, I explained the whole situation to him. As I was sobbing, I couldn't believe that I was crying to Jace over what happened with

Nick. The line was quiet when I stopped sobbing. I couldn't even tell how much time had passed by. I almost hung up thinking that was what he did, but he suddenly spoke, "Sugar, look up." I heard a knock on my car door and there he was. He listened to me and drove the whole way here. I couldn't believe he was here. He slowly opened my car door, embraced me in his warmth. I finally felt comforted, with Jace rubbing my back and whispering to me that everything would be okay. He was exactly what I needed. I needed his warmth and his strength because mine was dwindling. I was exactly where I was supposed to be. We stood there for a while, then decided to go inside.

Mom and Jenna still hadn't made it home. We decided to watch a movie. I couldn't tell you what the movie was about. I was too absorbed in Jace to care. His warmth enveloped me. He made me feel safe.

    Near the end of the movie, I heard the door handle jiggle and in walked Jenna and mom. Mom looked a bit surprised to see him here, Jenna looked like she fell in love. She batted her eye lashes and made her way over to Jace and me. "Hello?" She said as she held out her hand to him. "Jace." he said with that wickedly handsome grin of his. I figuratively saw my little sister melt. This was hilarious. I was stunned that someone actually could've had an effect on her, Oh My Gosh, she was atually speechless. "And I'm the mom" my mom added quite

A Minor Happy Ending

sarcastically jutting her hand in his direction. I giggled at her tone as did Jace, he reached for her hand and replied, "Pleased to meet you both." I was pretty sure both of them were impressed by the smile on their faces, which pleased me. The rest of the evening breezed by with relaxed conversation, Jace even helped mom with dinner. The night was perfect, as only Jace could make it. His easy going persona seemed to rub off on everyone. After dinner, Mom and Jenna retired to their rooms to prepare for tomorrow. Jenna whined about finishing math homework before departing the living room. She waved good bye to Jace with a silly grin and goo goo eyes to match. She almost ran into the wall trying to get one last peek at him before exiting the room.

"Well, I think that I have some competition" I said sounding defeated. "And she doesn't usually take no for an answer." He chuckled and quite dryly said, "She'll just have to learn patience and wait until you start showing some wear and tear. Then I can start all over with an exact replica!" My mouth dropped open, a small gasp left my mouth. Then when I gained my senses back, I grabbed his nipple through his t-shirt and twisted. "What was that?" I said feigning offense. His expression turned primal and he said, "What's good for the goose!" It took me a second to understand the meaning of his plans. Oh shit! That was when I hurried to my feet and made a run for it. I was out the door within seconds and he followed. He caught up with me quickly, by that time we were next to his car. He grabbed me by my waist, shoved me up against the car and pressed every rock hard inch of his body against mine. Our chests were heaving in sync with each other. He leaned in closer and whispered, "Now, Sugar was that nice?" unable to speak from the tension between us, I just shook my head. He leaned in closer, I felt his warm breathe on my lips and smelled the mint from his gum. As I leaned into his arms, his grip tightened, he raised one hand to my chin tilting it up to meet his gaze. His eyes so blue grew darker. I found lust and something else there. Then he whispered against my lips, "Come stay with me." It was a command not a question, everything in me made me want to comply. Before I could think twice, I whispered , "Okay" he released a breath and his whole body relaxed . He breathed me in,"I sleep better when you are there. I want you by my side, sugar." I felt treasured. Not that I'd ever wanted to be owned, but this felt good. I wanted to be his and him to be mine.

On the way to his place, anticipation and excitement fluttered in my belly. I wasn't sure if I was ready for the next step yet. I had wanted this for months, but we'd just became an us. Us. I loved the sound of us.

A Minor Happy Ending

As I was daydreaming, I felt like I was being watched. I looked over to find him staring at me with his cocky little grin in place. He grabbed my hand, brushed my knuckles against his lips causing a shiver throughout my body and his grin broadened. "What ya thinkin about Sugar?" with a knowing look in his eyes. I felt my face warm. "Oh, it must be good from the color of your face" he drawled so easily. I felt the warmth spread throughout my body as he continued, "I love your reaction to me." The rest of the ride he continued to keep rubbing my knuckles across his lips like he was sneaking a taste of his favorite dessert. He pulled into his driveway, that excitement in my belly returned. He got out of the car and carried my bag into the house.

The house was so still that it appeared abandoned if it weren't for the immaculate landscaping and sterility of the home. It didn't have that home like feel that I got when I walked into my house. Although now, when Jace encircled his arms around me from behind, that was where I found my home. Within a matter of seconds, I went from feeling utterly uncomfortable to finding the place I was meant to be. He turned me to face him and brushed a soft kiss to my lips for what seemed like a wonderful eternity. "Dyl, I'm so glad you came. I'm not ready to leave you yet." I answered with a small peck to his lips then he led me to his room.

He sat my bag on his bed and headed to the adjoining bathroom. I started to pull out my silk boxers and tank to sleep in for the night when I felt him come up from behind me. He wrapped one arm around my waist and nuzzled my neck, causing a giggle to erupt. "I could listen to that all day" he said and continued the precious torture . Even though it tickled, I felt the tightness in my belly, the warmth spread between my legs. My breathing began to quicken, I turned and attacked his mouth with mine urgently. His response mirrored mine. It felt like we are trying to climb each other. I couldn't get close enough. I wanted closer. I began to pull at his shirt and raise it above his head, he complied willingly. I found the most beautiful set of tan abs with that V-shaped area near his narrow hips, I rubbed them lightly with my hands. The only thing that I thought of at that moment was that I wanted a taste of them. I lowered myself to my knees, on my way I began to lick his chest, his hard abs, and then I traced his impressive V with my tongue. I looked up to gauge his reaction when I was met with hooded eyes looking admiringly at me. He began stroking my hair, telling me how beautiful I was, making me want to please him even more. My hands reached for his jeans and felt the strain behind his zipper, I slowly peeled the zipper down to free him. HOLY HELL, he went commando! He made sure to be ready for me as he would be surprised to find the same

A Minor Happy Ending

from me. I reached in to grab him, impressive was not the right word to describe what I found in his pants. His length alone threatened my oral skills, let alone the girth. But I'd never been one to back down from a challenge. When I pulled him out, placed him in my mouth, I couldn't get enough of the taste of him. Masculine yet sweet on my tongue, knowing that I was causing him so much pleasure turned me on even more. I licked the tip and continued. His groans of pleasure caused a reaction in me that I didn't expect. I began feasting on him and taking him as deep as I could , using my hand to make up for what my mouth couldn't handle. Lost in the feeling and emotions of giving my man pleasure, I felt his hands tightening in my hair causing a moan from me, he hardened even more in my mouth. Then all of a sudden he abruptly pulled away, picked me up and began kissing me fiercely. He began ripping off my clothes to find that I'd also gone commando, a feral groan slipped from his lips.

He started to lower his jeans to the floor and whispered, "I want a taste first Dyl and then I want to feel your warmth around me squeezing me until we both scream each others names. I want tonight to be the one and only memory that comes to mind when you think of making love for the first time. This is the only first that matters. Me and you, Dyl. Just us." He lowered me onto the bed appreciating all my curves and valleys, that he licked and nipped on his way between my legs, he inhaled deeply . He whispered against my sex, "You smell so sweet" Surprised at my ease with him, I opened my legs wider and felt his warm breath against my sex. I began to squirm when he clamped his strong arms across my legs holding me in place. I felt his tongue apply warm pressure against my sex with expertise causing my hips to buck, but he still held me in place to absorb all the pleasure that he was giving. When he started fucking his tongue in and out, my body began to quiver. When I thought that I couldn't take anymore, he sucked my clit into his mouth and punished it with his rapid tongue movements causing me to tumble over the edge in pure ecstasy. The sound that resonated from my throat couldn't be described as human. When I came down from my Jace high, I found him climbing up my body, kissing my little nooks in the crease of my thigh, the valley between my breasts, and the curve of my neck until his lips landed on mine. He kissed me fiercely while my scent and his mingled. The combination was intoxicating and addictive. His lips left mine for a brief moment to reach into the bedside table. My head was so clouded with lust, all I heard was a ripping noise, then I looked down to see him roll the condom onto his impressive length. He looked into my eyes questioning if I was ready for the next step in our journey and with a slight nod of my head, we became one. I watched his beautiful face as he slowly entered me,

A Minor Happy Ending

inch by inch. It was the most delicious torture I'd ever felt. My eyes never left his gaze filled with lust and wonder. He looked tortured, yet blissful every time he entered and withdrew from my body. "You fit me Dyl, the softest perfect fucking fit! Nothing has ever felt better baby!" With those words, I tipped over the edge yelling out, "Jace!" I felt myself clamp around his girth, his thrusting became more urgent as he chased his own release. I felt his whole body tighten as his release took him over, saying my name and covering me with his perfect torso. As his breathing slowed, he lifted his head and kissed every inch of my face and whispered, "Beautiful" a kiss to my forehead, "Sweet" a kiss to my cheek, "Amazing" a kiss to the corner of my lips, and "My love" a kiss behind my ear.

As we lied there tangled and in complete bliss, Jace broke the silence "So Dyl, you can show yourself out now" he said nonchalantly as if I was some whore off the street. Fire burned in my belly, I was so furious I was about to grab him by his balls if he wasn't still inside me. I snapped back, "Well you couldn't even wait ..." I was interrupted by a goofy chuckle coming from the asshole still inside me. "And what's so fucking funny?" I snapped as he began to trail kisses along my neck, I attempted to wiggle free. "Sugar I'm just playing with you. I want you in my bed with me for as long as you'll have me. But I do have to go get rid of something and I'll be right back." My anger and anxiety dissipated as I realized that he just had a terrible sense of humor. This was the most amazing sex I'd ever had. I had to admit that my heart fluttered when he said that he wanted me around as long as I'd have him. Right now, I wanted him always.

  He rose up and headed to the bathroom to dispose of the condom. I watched his muscles move as he made it back to the bed, slipped behind me and dragged me close to him. He placed his head in my neck inhaling my scent and whispered, "Dyl, you mean more to me than you'll ever know baby. You are all I want." My chest filled with love for this man professing his affections for me. "I know baby, me too. You're more." I proclaimed not able to say aloud the whole truth in fear of scaring him away. I loved him. I loved the tenderness he gave, I loved his terrible sense of humor, I loved how he looked at me like I was the most precious thing he'd ever seen, and I loved most of all, the way we were when we were together. Everything was just better. With my confession, I allowed my body to relax and drifted off into dreamland.

Chapter 16

The next few days consisted of Jace and I huddled up in our own personal sanctuary of his home. He made me breakfast every morning. We watched old movies. He played the guitar for me. I was pretty sure he liked seeing my lusty gazes when he played, imagining those talented fingers running all over my body instead of all over those strings. I was such a flippin groupie! Just Jace's groupie though.

 I got texts periodically from my girls checking up on me. Max texted me that she loved me and was sorry that Nick and I didn't work out and to visit her soon. I told her that I'd text her when I got home tomorrow.

Our little bubble we'd been in the last couple of days would be deflated tomorrow morning, because Jace's parents returned from their trip and he would rather introduce me the traditional way. He'd already made plans for me to come over for dinner in a couple of days. He seemed so excited, but I was nervous as hell. By overhearing some of his conversations with them, his voice was tense and he seemed on edge while on the phone, so I was fearful of what I'd see in person.

As if he knew I was thinking of him, he walked in with his easy smile. His jeans riding low on his hips and his black concert shirt, he looked sexier than hell, all I wanted to do was jump on him. "Well, hello Sugar." He said as he joined me on the couch cuddling up beside me, wrapping his strong arms around me. "I don't want you to go" he whined huskily then began to nibble my ears. I squirmed and giggled as I ran my hand through his short hair. "I don't want to go either baby, but it'll actually give you a chance to miss me." I replied between giggles. "I haven't seen my friends too much lately. In fact we haven't left your house except for work in 3 days! We can't become hermits now." He drew me closer, nuzzled my neck, and whispered, "I'm perfectly happy right here with you. I don't need to be anywhere else. I think I'll just duct tape you naked to my bed and keep you there until we are eighty. I'll make sure it's quite pleasurable for you!" he said in the most seductive voice. Jovially I remarked "I'm so sure you will Mr. Harvey, but some of us need to work. Not sit around playing the guitar and looking quite sexy all day, I need to pay for college this fall." He flinched at my comment. His hold loosened, he leaned back on the couch

A Minor Happy Ending

brooding. "Is that what you really think of me, Dyl?" he asked looking sad and thoughtful. "No baby, I didn't mean that at all. I thought we were playing around." His face still thoughtful, but that grin began to make an appearance again, making my heart do that stupid little flutter thing again. "But I do think that you are quite sexy." His arms snaked around me again pulling me onto his lap when he replied, "As are you my love, as are you." Love, there was that word again. I wondered if he really meant it or if he was one of those people who were liberal with the word, like I love ice cream or footy pajamas. I knew sometimes I could be a little forward and jump into things, but I knew I loved him. It was crazy, we'd only been together for almost a week. How could I possibly be in love with this man already? Maybe we needed this time apart to make sure our feelings were real. "What has you thinking so hard Sugar? You look like your trying to solve a puzzle, everything ok?" His sexy voice brought me out of my fog, I'd always been quick on my feet, so I came up with a little white lie. "I was thinking what it'll be like without you sleeping next to me." We sat and held each other for a little while until I heard a little chirp notifying me of a text message. I looked down to find a text from Max.

Max: *Earth to Dyl! Earth to Dyl!*

Me: *Hi baby girl! I'm here.*

Max: *Have you come out off your orgasm cloud long enough to spend time with your girls?*

Me: *Ya, I'm free tonight. Miss me that much, huh?*

Max: *Well duh crazy hoe! Cam's house tonight 8pm. You can even bring the boy toy!*

Ugh, Cam's house. The mere thought of her made me cringe. I didn't know if I could stomach her right now, but I did miss Max and Jade. I guess if Jace was with me I could deal with her for a little while.

Me: *Ok. 8 it is.*

This would be our first night out with all of our friends as a couple. I wasn't sure that I wanted the whole clan around us. We were happy in our little bubble. I didn't want anyone to taint our bubble. But we had to face them sooner or later, so I guess sooner it was. "Dyl, Is everything ok?" Jace asked with concern. I responded robotically, "Yep, we were invited to Cam's tonight by Max. She misses me. She said to bring you too, so that's a good sign, huh?" He

A Minor Happy Ending

must've heard the weariness in my tone, because he pulled me back, looked into my eyes and asked. "Do you want to go to Cam's?" The answer was, not really, but I had to face them. So I nodded feigning enthusiasm. He saw right through me and said, "Don't worry Sugar, Cam won't bother you. I've known her for a long time. She may be selfish, but she probably feels bad about the whole situation." But he didn't see the hatred I saw in her eyes while she was riding on my ex boyfriends cock like it was the bull ride at the fair. She reveled in the fact that I caught them. She got some sick pleasure out of seeing the surprise and hurt on my face. I guess I'd trust that Jace was right and tried to move forward.

"C'mon babe, let's get going so we can drop off my things. I can change before we head to Cam's." Reluctantly I let all the frustration go and hoped that tonight wasn't awkward as hell. "Ok Sugar, let's go eat some home cookin!" he exclaimed in a goofy fake southern accent. He seemed genuinely excited for a home cooked meal. I hated to tell him that it was probably Tater tot casserole or Tuna noodle surprise. Neither my mom nor I were chefs in the making.

We gathered my things and his guitar, headed for home.

Chapter 17

    After mom's great Tuna noodle surprise, which Jace seemed to really enjoy. We sat around the table. He entertained Jenna, talking about their favorite bands. He made her blush by humming a few tunes to her at the table, in which she turned three shades of red and batted her little eyelashes. Oh her poor future boyfriend had a lot to live up to! Poor guy! Who could blame her! He was amazing, funny, sweet and holy hell, that man made my body convulse like an epileptic in a disco. I'd never had so many orgasms in such a short time. I was surprised I wasn't dehydrated from the flooding he caused between my thighs. And he was mine. All mine and he only wanted me. Hee Hee. I checked my cell and noticed we needed to be at Cam's soon. I stood and Jace's eyes followed me. "I'm just going to go freshen up before we go." He nodded and returned to entertaining his biggest fan. I went to my closet to pick out a new outfit, mom followed. "He's nice

A Minor Happy Ending

Dyl, really nice." She said sounding pleased. But then her face turned serious and said, "Just don't rush anything; you have all summer before you go to college. He's smitten, kitten I can tell, but you guys are young and have plenty of time for serious later. I'm glad you're happy. I love you baby girl!" "Thanks, mom." I squeaked out trying not to over think our relationship. I wanted to tell her that I loved him already, but decided not to, didn't want to worry her. I dressed into a pair of skinny jeans that hugged my curves and a graphic tee that showed a sliver of tummy. I topped off my outfit with a pair of flipflops. Good thing I just painted the toes. My comfort gear to face our friends, but why did I feel like I was headed into the lion's den.

Jace and I arrived at Cam's and it looked like the usual crew was there. Smith and Max were on the porch sitting closely. They were talking and cuddling like a new couple. It was sweet. I liked seeing Max happy. We exited the Century and met in front of the car. My whole body tensed, because I really didn't want to be there right then. As if he knew exactly what I was thinking, Jace grasped my hand and entwined his fingers with mine. My body began to relax, with his hand in mine I gathered the courage to move ahead. As we made our way closer to the porch, Max noticed me. At first she had a confused look on her face, but then the biggest smile grew across her lips and she yelled out, "Dyl, you crazy hoe I missed you so much!" as she ran toward me and gave me a tight squeeze around the ribs. "I missed you too Maxwell!" as I wrapped my arms around her too. She was my sister and I missed her. We'd never spent more than a day apart since her parents passed away, I was one of the few guarantees she had in life. I wasn't going anywhere. She let go of me, assessed Jace and my entwined fingers then looked him in the eyes and said, "Listen pretty boy, if you hurt my girl, your boys are gone! Got it!" gesturing to his balls. Jace's cocky grin appeared and he said, "Wouldn't think of it! Plus I'm rather fond of the boys thanks! I'm glad Dyllan has you to protect her." Feeding Max's need to be needed. I looked to Max for direction when she smiled and said, "Jace can I talk with Dyl, a sec?" He nodded, headed onto the porch and greeted Smith with the traditional bro handshake half hug thing. Max pulled me aside and said, "What happened between you and Nick, is just that. I don't want anything weird between us Dyl. We've been friends for too long, okay? It seems like you both messed up. I just hope you can respect Cam and Nick "dating" and I told them that they needed to respect you and Jace. I understand that it may be awkward as shit, but it is what it is. I'm not picking sides, I love you all." I was instantly fuming mad, "Who the fuck told you to pick sides? I sure as fuck wouldn't. That slut rag! I never would ask you to choose! You

A Minor Happy Ending

should've fucking seen her Max! When I walked in that crazy bitch's eyes were fixed on me and grinning while fucking him. It was like she planned it all along! Ugh, what a bitch!" Wow that felt good. I must've needed to get that out! "And where were you Dyl, what were you doing? Because you weren't fucking your boyfriend, who were you with Dyl?" she shot venomously at me. My eyes widened in shock and gasped. Sadly I replied, "Not fucking anyone, but not where I probably should've been until I ended things with Nick, your right Maxwell. I'm no saint, but it felt like she was attacking me personally, ya know. Shit Max that was a bit far, even for Cam. Next thing ya know, she'll try to steal you and Jade too! I know I wasn't innocent when it came to Nick, but I did try. It was a hard decision to make and I didn't want to hurt either of you. I just fucked it all up." She grabbed my head and stared into my eyes for a second. She pulled me into her arms and hugged me so tightly that I felt like I was losing my breath. She whispered, "I know you'd never purposely hurt me or Nick, but you also need to not be afraid to tell me things. You're my best friend Dyl. No one can take your place, my sister from another mister!" With that comment, a stray tear landed on her shoulder, she pulled me back to look in my eyes again. "Now let's stop all this blubbery mess and go have fun with our friends. Oh and by the way, Smith and I are kind of dating now. I didn't want to say anything until I knew for sure because I didn't want things to be awkward." She said with a blush as her gaze travelled to the porch where Smith was sitting with Jace. "Awe, my girl is growing up!" I said watching the redness creep up into her cheeks. She proceeded to tell me how they ended up becoming an official couple that night after they left Club 43. She said that Smith attempted to drop Cam off at her house, but Cam said she didn't want to end the night yet. So, they decided to extend the party to Max's place. Max, Cam and Smith shared a joint in the car before going in the house. She said they began drinking when Nick came out of his room and joined in. She said that she could tell that he was brooding and thought a fun time would be good for him. She said that the next thing she knew Cam was asleep on the couch and Nick went to bed. She and Smith were still awake, she knew this was the time to make her move. Smith was shy, she knew that she would be waiting forever if she left it up to him. When she became tired she told him that she was going to bed. She went to hug him goodnight and decided to just go for it and kissed him. She admitted that it wasn't the first time, they snuck kisses before when everyone else paired up, but that time it felt more real. She said it took everything in her to ask him to go to her room with her, but it was the best thing that she did. She told me that he made her so happy and I could tell that he did. She was glowing. I admitted to her what I saw that morning and was so happy for her. She smiled, nodded and said, "Okay crab apple let's go hang out with the fellas!" I followed her up the steps and sat in the seat next to Max. "So, who's here tonight?" I asked attempting to prepare myself for whatever was to come. Jace grabbed my hands, laced our fingers and rested them in his lap rubbing the back of my hand in small circles, calming me. I didn't know how he always knew when I needed his comfort. Max replied sheepishly but simultaneously attempting to reassure me, "Well Jade, Cam and Nick are inside. Jade's friend Lisa is on her way. We thought that we could order pizza watch scary movies and then later we can head to The Diner for some coffee and dessert. Sound good?" Jace squeezed my hand for support and I nodded. I could never say no to Max. Jace leaned in and whispered in my ear, "If it gets weird, we'll just leave Sugar. I'm here you'll be fine." I believed him. It felt weird to allow myself to rely on a man, but I'd rely on Jace. I looked at Max and nodded, "Let's do this babe!" She gave me a weird look and returned my nod with one of her own and replied, "Wow Jace I never thought I'd see the day Dyl let a man take care of her!" Then turned to Jace and said, "Don't forget my warning bucko!" I knew her warning was meant to be serious, but she was so tiny it was hard not to giggle. "Hey!" she replied when I could no longer stifle my laughter. I blew her a kiss and gestured toward the door.

Max lead the way into Cam's apartment and announced our arrival. Jade and Cam were sitting on the couch probably overanalyzing a simple situation because that was what new graduates did, since we were convinced that we knew everything about everything. My mom told me that the older you got, you realized you really didn't know much of anything. Jade turned around and had a smile for me, but Cam looked like the cat that ate the canary. Oh I knew what she did, even if no one else believed me. She plastered her best fake smile to her face and waved at us. Max and Jade fell for her plastic façade, so I had to play along too. I was just going to be a lot more careful around her. Jace was right on my back, I felt him become instantly rigid causing my body to tense as well. That was when I heard Nick enter the room, he was stumbling and his face paled. He looked clouded and when his eyes met mine, hurt and confusion washed over his face. He clumsily plopped on the couch between Cam and Jade, leaned into Cam whispering in her ear, but his eyes never left mine. My stomach performed somersaults and I was annoyed. Is he high? He looked really high. He'd only smoked twice before and he couldn't even handle it then. He told me once that he didn't really like the way it made him feel. He liked to be in control. This was my fault. I did this! Before I could think, I blurted, "Are you high?" All of them began

A Minor Happy Ending

to chuckle and Cam spoke up, "Why yes Miss Pott, the kettle is black." in her most snide condescending tone of voice. I chose not to let her get the best of me and replied, "Was just asking, do what ya want." Nick finally decided to speak for himself, "I sure did!" as he grabbed Cam and placed her on his lap. He began nibbling on her neck, but kept his eyes on me the entire time. Well it looked like Cam got to him too. It was what it was. I kept repeating to myself to keep my normally short fuse at bay, but they were making it difficult. I felt my body become rigid, as Jace's grip tightened on my hand. I was pulled backwards and somehow ended up on Jace's lap on the love seat. My body relaxed as he began rubbing my back and asked Smith, "So, what movie are we watching kids?" After that I was lost in the whole insane situation in front of me. Why didn't we just stay in our bubble? Our happy bubble that no one could ruin, it was only ours. Now, I was stuck in a house with an evil witch who wanted to steal my life. I had no choice but to play her game if I wanted to keep my friends. Jade brought me out of my cloud when she jumped up to sit next to me and Jace. "What up hoe?" I smiled and hugged my friend. She whispered as we embraced, "I told you that she'd be fine. Granted both of you royally fucked up, but at least it wasn't just you. She really likes him, ya know?" she said nodding toward Cam and Nick. I let her talk, but I did't believe a word, Jade could be tricked too. She was less naïve than Max, but she liked Cam and would believe her. I watched the two of them out of the corner of my eye. She played her game well. When she caught me watching she would grab his face and kiss him. He responded like any normal man, with a groan and returned sentiment. She continued assaulting his mouth until I looked away and she came up for air giggling and said loudly, "Oh baby I just can't help myself around you. You make me want you all the time!" My blood was boiling. Not because I wanted Nick back, but because she was using him to get to me. She hated me for some reason. I felt like I was losing my mind. Why would she hate me? It wasn't adding up. Jade tapped on my leg and said, "He's been high and drunk all day. He came over early this afternoon and he and Cam haven't stopped. I think he's still hurt over you Dyl. Just let him have this for now then we will kick his ass in a couple days." I nodded and smiled at my friend. I turned my attention to my reason to be happy and found him looking concerned for me. I knew he was doing his best to comfort and protect me. That filled my heart with so much love for this man, I remembered his warm mouth on me, kissing me senseless. I felt a blush rise from my chest and settled in my cheeks. A wicked grin was on his face since he somehow always knew exactly what I was thinking about. He had this uncanny ability to read my reactions. I would

A Minor Happy Ending

almost believe that he could read my thoughts, but I didn't want to know. I didn't want to sensor my thoughts of Jace. He leaned in and whispered so only I could hear, "I miss our bubble Sugar. I miss your sweet taste and being wrapped around your sweet curves." I forgot where I was for a minute, my lips met his in a soft embrace for just a moment before I pulled away, looked into those beautiful blue eyes and saw what I'd been looking for all night. My home. He'd been with me the whole time. With that knowledge, I finally had the nerve to go on with this cluster fuck of a night and put on my party girl pants. "Well, I have an idea, why don't we say fuck the movie and head to Jades and have a bonfire? What ya think, Jade?" Jade shrugged and she smiled noncommittally when Max jumped on the band wagon, "That sounds amazing! Everyone in?" Everybody agreed, even Nick which surprised me since his eyes hadn't left my face since I caught him watching me kiss Jace. Jace saw it too, I thought. He looked at him with sympathy not annoyance or jealousy, which made me love him even more. He was amazing. We all agreed to pick up some goodies for the bonfire and meet at Jades in an hour. Jade said that she had a few tents, we could camp out for the night, so no one would have to drive home. I texted my mom telling her the situation. She appreciated the call and the notice. Jade, her friend Lisa and Jace rode with me, the rest rode in

Smith's car. After we gathered our sleeping bags, we stopped by the store for S'more ingredients and pie filling. Then Jace grabbed pizza sauce, cheese and pepperoni. When I asked him for what he said campfire pizzas with such excitement that I thought I might burst into laughter. Sometimes the simplest things made him so happy. I was so glad one of those things was me.

A Minor Happy Ending

Chapter 18

When we arrived at Jade's, Jace unloaded the car as we girls said hello to Jades parents and thanked them for allowing us to stay. As always, Jade's mom told us to be careful and Jade's dad told us to keep those men in line. When we returned outside, Max and the rest were there, but Max didn't look happy at the moment. I saw Nick and Jace standing nose to nose, both of their bodies as rigid as stone. If I wasn't so concerned right now, I would've totally been turned on! The testosterone in the air was insane. I didn't even hesitate to step between them when Nick went to shove Jace, his hands landed on me. I felt my body jolt backwards, landing on something hard and unyielding. The ache began in my back and then grew to my shoulders and neck. I was shocked, but I wasn't hurt. I might've been sore in the morning. The next thing I heard was, "FUCK! God baby, I'm so sorry. Why did you run in between us like that?" Nick said as he attempted to wrap his arms around me, but then I felt Jace knock his hands away. As he wrapped his arms around me and growled low in his throat. He actually growled and I swore that I heard him say mine. Holy hell that never happened before, I'd never felt more protected. Nick took a step back, hung his head realizing what he said and apologized again. I told him that I was fine and I forgave him. Jace tensed at my words, whispered that we needed to talk. He pulled me aside and said, "We are leaving or you are going to let me beat his fucking ass for touching you!" My mouth dropped open from the intensity of his statement. This was not my Jace. My Jace was free and easy. I took a cleansing breath and spoke, "Baby, he didn't mean to hurt me. He's not himself. He's high. He just lost his girlfriend and he's fucking a troll!" at that comment a tiny smirk appeared on his lips. "Think of how you would feel, babe. Let's give him the benefit of doubt. It will be fine, you'll see. How did your little tiff start anyway?" He shrugged and shook his head. "No reason really, don't worry about it. I guess I can give that asshole a break because if I lost you Dyl, there would be no recovery for me." My eyes widened, he grabbed me and kept me there for a while. I wasn't sure what to do, I'd never felt like this for anyone else, so in pure Dyllan fashion I blurted, "I've never felt like this before." So much for taking it slow and easy like mom suggested. I might as well had told him that I loved him. Yet again I jumped in

A Minor Happy Ending

with both feet, but I'd never been more sure either. He grabbed my face, stared into my eyes and his crooked smile showed itself. Then his mouth descended upon mine giving me every bit of emotion that he had in him, I took it all. His feelings for me poured through his kiss, as well as his lust, tenting his pants. We stayed there for a little while longer kissing and holding one another until we heard everyone talking by the fire. The tents were already set up, the fire was blazing. We walked over to everyone hand in hand with the biggest smiles on our faces. We found a way to bring our bubble along.

We spent the rest of the evening sitting by the fire, telling stories of our pasts. Nick drowned himself with beer and ignored everyone. His eyes wandered my way from time to time, I had attempted to give him a reassuring smile, but it was still too early for that. He didn't want my pity. He was hurt and confused. Maybe this wasn't such a good idea. My shoulders began to tense and per usual Jace could tell and began to rub my shoulders, giving Nick a careful stare. It was strange feeling both sets of eyes on me at the same time. Nick suddenly jumped up and announced that he was going to bed, Cam wasn't far behind as she waved goodnight to Max and gave me her smug smirk. The rest of us sat a little longer cuddled up as couples, even Jade and Lisa. I wasn't reading too much into this yet, but I thought something was going on there, if Jade had something to tell us, she would. That was how our friendship worked. No labels, no judgement, and no limits! We were family. Jade asked Jace if he would play his guitar for us and he agreed. While he went to the car to retrieve his guitar, Jade said, "Wow Dyl the way he looks at you is melting my undies, shit girl! That is one sexy man. So, how exactly is this working out? Is he as stinking rich as Cam says? Are his parents snooty as fuck? Does he have a gold plated condom dispenser?" I had to chuckle at that comment. She was always so colorful. I loved Jade. I whispered in return, "His parents are definitely well off, but they are never there and you couldn't tell it by talking with him. He is so down to earth and easy to be with. And you have no idea how well he can melt a set of undies!" I was interrupted by a chuckle behind me and I felt the blush rise in my cheeks when I heard my man say, "Is that so? I definitely had to perform an inspection of your undies later for any apparent meltage!" Oh shit that was embarrassing! Only me! Jade and Max boisterously laughed, Lisa and Smith quietly chuckled to spare me any further embarrassment. Jace leaned down and kissed my cheek softly, then sat next to me with his guitar on his lap. Jade clapped her hands and told him to play anything that came to mind. He began to play that same rock ballad again and I honestly felt like I was going to swoon. I, Dyllan Prescott, did not normally swoon, but for him I would. His calloused fingers glided

A Minor Happy Ending

over those strings with ease, his gravely voice relaxed every muscle in my body. His lust filled blue eyes were on me the whole time. And man does that feel good. When the song ended he immediately began to play another song and seemed to get lost in it.

The smell of your skin, the warmth of your touch
I could breath you in, if it weren't too much
I watch from afar waiting for you to see
That the only one for you is me
Your fake smiles and feigned love for him don't fool this fool
But everyone else's eyes are covered by your brand of wool
Your are the master if deception, the magician of play
You make me love you more the longer you stay
When I see you with him the deception is clear to me
You are forcing things, not meant to be
I watch from afar waiting for you to see
That the only one for you is me
Please stop pleasing everyone and let me please you
Wanting my hands and my mouth all over you
But I'm waiting for you to realize what you can't see
He wasn't made for you, stop forcing things not meant to be
When we are together it's so easy
I watch from afar waiting for you to see

The only one for you is me
Until that day comes I fill my days with who I can
Why waste time when I know who I am
I'm in love with you and that's no lie
Your smile, your laughter, your kindest you show
Your loyalty, your strength, I live to watch you glow
So until your mine, I watch from afar waiting for you to see
What we can be
The only one for you is me.

Those soulful words filled me with longing. I wondered how long he waited for me. His words made me love him more. His voice was soul filled and would steal anyone's heart. I could listen to him for days. And he was mine and he loved me! Holy cow this man loved me! He didn't exactly tell me though. Maybe I'd wait to confess my feelings to him, until I knew for sure where he stood. A song wouldn't be as good if it was wishy washy. I looked up to find my friends mesmerized by my mans talent as well as I was. So, not only was he amazing looking, he was amazing in bed, and now amazingly talented.

Max spoke up first, "Wow you got it bad, man!" and nodded in approval to Jace. Jade gave him a thumbs up while Lisa golf clapped for him in her sweet way. When his

A Minor Happy Ending

eyes met mine, he looked apprehensive and asked, "What'd ya think Sugar?" He looked down like he was preparing to hear my answer, I hesitated to make sure that I said the right words, "I loved it baby, it was amazing." I continued in jest, "So, who's this chick you were totally in love with?" acting the fool. His apprehension was replaced with pure bliss as his grin spread across his entire face. "Oh, she's a total smart ass!" I smacked his arm in retaliation and smiled. Next he leaned in, whispered in my ear, "And I'm completely in love with her." My eyes widened in awe of this man who was pouring his heart out to me, I replied quietly for only him to hear, "I'm in love with you." I said it so matter-of-fact like there could've been no other truth. That was when his gaze heated, we leaned in toward each other and slowly his lips brushed against mine. He began to add more pressure causing me to want more and I all but climbed him, when the sound of a throat clearing caused us to pause. Jade spoke up, "Easy there kids, no one wants to watch y'all tasting tonsils!" We all began laughing. When the laughter died down, so did the fire. Then we decided to call it a night.

Chapter 19

    Jace and I had our own dome tent. We zipped our sleeping bags together to made one large bag. As we got settled for the night, Jace wrapped his arms around me and held me close, so my head was resting in his neck, while he was rubbing circles along my side. "Sugar, did you mean it?" he asked almost sounding child like. "Mean what babe?" I asked him with a smile. "Love me?" he repeated again sheepishly. I replied directly, "More than I understand right now." The broad smile that spread across those beautiful lips, floored me. His arms snaked around me and he spent the next hour humming my song until I drifted off to sleep. I could've done this forever.
A few hours later, I awoke because I had to pee. I slid out of Jace's arms, headed towards the out house behind the barn. I didn't like the out house, but it was better than going behind a tree, at least it had toilet paper. I did my business and opened the door to find Nick sitting there, he

A Minor Happy Ending

tentatively looked up at me and asked, " Well is it true? Did you fake it with me?" I must've given him a confused expression because his tone was more fierce, "The song Dyl. I see the way you look at him. You never looked at me that way. Ugh, I love you so much." That little speech made my heart drop into my stomach. "You didn't do anything wrong Nick. You were wonderful to me. I just didn't fall in love with you. I didn't fake anything, it killed me to hurt you Nick." His shoulders drooped, a tear fell down his cheek when he whispered, "If he screws up, I'll be there! I can see you really care for this guy and he seems to care for you. I'll always love you." The hurt expression on his face was breaking my heart all over again, even after all his douchebag antics. I replied quickly, "Thanks Nick." I added, "Can you lay off the partying, you are way better than that." A small grin was on his lips and he said, "Yea, it's kind of wearing me out. I better get back." I whispered, "Yea, me too." We made our way back to our own tents. Me to my man. Him to the nasty troll bitch! What? It wasn't like she didn't deserve it. Ok, that was the last one.
For tonight anyway.
I crawled back inside the tent into Jace's arms where I was supposed to be.

The next morning we all went to The Diner for breakfast and prepared to part ways. Nick and Jace were civil with each other, obviously for my sake. The girls and I bantered about the new movie we wanted to go see next weekend, the guys just listened to our jibber jabber, shaking their heads at our crazy off the wall humor. In the back of my mind, the lingering feeling that something wasn't right was plaguing me. Maybe because I was about to spend the next few days without Jace. His parents were back in town and they'd like to spend time with him.

We'd spent the last week together. I didn't get annoyed or bored with him like some of my exes. When I was around him, I felt empowered, sexy, and fulfilled.

We all piled in the Century and I drove everyone home, saving Jace for last. I was keeping him with me for as long as I could. We drove to his house with our fingers intertwined and a thickness in the air. I didn't want to sound like a whiny girlfriend, but I didn't want to sleep without him. I'd miss his smell, his warmth, and his strong arms holding me. I slept better with him there. Now I gathered my control and muttered in my fake southern accent, "Now what are you ever going to do without little ole me around?" He chuckled with that raspy voice that made my insides quiver with excitement. I loved when I caused his laughter. "Well sugar" he mustered his own version of a southern accent which I found incredibly sexy, "I just don't want to find out! Let's just runaway together and never look back. Me and you and the open road.

A Minor Happy Ending

Twenty four seven. I'll play my guitar for gas money and you can just sit there and look beautiful." Man wouldn't I had loved for that to happen. As long as I was with Jace, I would've been home. "Not so fast hot stuff, I earn my own way! Even though I love the compliment I definitely can take care of myself." With a twinkle in his eyes that he usually got when he was thinking dirty thoughts, he grabbed a hold of me from across the middle console and pulled me onto his lap. "Dyllan, did you forget that you belong to me? It's my job to take care of you. Sugar, your sweetness is all mine!" He said jovially, but with a tone making it quite clear that he was testing my boundaries. "Well babe, I'd hate to tell ya, but your all mine! It means I take care of you too." I stared into his blue eyes to see his admiration. He stared back and steadied himself with a breathe like he was about to confess something and then he shook his head and smiled. "Not sure what to do with you sugar! You make me crazy." He stated with emotion in the back of his throat. I searched his face trying to find the secrets he was hiding, but realized he has already told me enough for now. I wasn't going to push him, he'd tell me when he was ready. I ignored the nagging feeling to investigate further. Instead, I kissed him reassuringly, then the heat between us had risen. The next thing I knew I was straddling his lap and his hands were in my hair, kissing me like this was our last. I pulled away, placed my head in his neck and breathed in Jace. I couldn't shake this feeling no matter what I tried, but it was probably just in my head. He didn't want me to go, I could tell that he wasn't too excited about his parents coming home. It would be great if we could've just lived in our bubble. The bubble that no one else could fit into. Our bubble was pretty hard to pop. He held me for a while, we listened to each other breathe. I didn't want to leave him, but I could just imagine his parents coming home tomorrow and catching us in his bed. Not so sure that would make a great impression. 'Well hello Mr and Mrs Harvey, your son just gave me about five orgasms and I worship the ground he walks on!' Hmmm didn't quite think that would've worked out well. I chuckled and Jace pushed me away to look in my eyes curiously and said, "What?" He smiled and produced a chuckle from the back of his throat. "Not gonna tell me, huh?" His hands found my ribs and tickled. He was relentless with his hands that tortured me in both good and bad ways. I wiggled on his lap giggling and then it happened.

My jaw dropped open!

A Minor Happy Ending

I farted!

Oh my God, I could not believe I did that! He stopped abruptly and had this incredulous look on his face. I felt my face heat up, I could've probably won a bet right now guessing that my face was 10 different shades of red. I was so stunned, I was speechless. I had nothing! No quick witted comment, no clever quip, just silence. He stared at me for a few more seconds, but seemed like a lifetime, then lowered his head. Awe shit! Was he mad at me for this? Ya know what, he did it, he kept tickling me. Is he repulsed by me now? Ugh. Then I noticed a slight motion in his shoulders moving up and down, then the movements increased in speed. His ears were turning red. Oh my God was he holding his breath? I couldn't even smell anything. Was he that revolted by me? Out of pure frustration and embarrassment, I attempted to move back into the drivers seat when I felt his arms tighten around me, he could no longer hide his feelings. He burst with a loud guffaw and proceeded to laugh with his entire body causing the car to shake. Then said, "Sugar, did you hear that frog? It was the loudest croak I've ever heard!" He said while looking up at me with his blue eyes. Embarrassed, I made a mad dash for the door and ran out of the Century. He chased me out the door, when I felt his arms wrap around me from behind dragging me back to his hard chest. I willingly gave in. He kissed my neck while whispering in my ear, "Our bubble as you call it?" I nodded. "Nothing can break it." he said seriously. Then added, "and hey if you keep doing that, it may float!" On that note I tried to run off again, but his grip tightened. He began to trail kisses from behind my ear, down my neck, and onto my shoulder. His hands began to roam and grasped my hips, then my waist. He quickly turned me, backing me up against the car and pressed his hard length against me. I loved that I did that to him. It was such a rush knowing that it was just me. He wanted me. My hands roamed everywhere on his torso until they landed on the waistband of his jeans. Halting myself there so we weren't arrested for indecent exposure. I allowed him to own me, consume me, and love me. I felt it. So when we came up for air I voiced it. "I love you Jace Harvey," I said with conviction. His crooked grin appeared, he repeated the endearment back. We stayed there for what seemed like hours holding each other as he hummed my song to me. Both of us dreading the next week when his parents were home. Eventually we said goodnight.

I pulled into my drive way and saw that the living room light was on. Mom must've been up reading. I got out of the a Century and headed for the door when my phone buzzed.

Jace: *text me when u make it home, so I know u r ok*

A Minor Happy Ending

Me: *home*

Jace: *already Dyl!*

Then my phone rang. "Hello.." I was quickly interrupted, "God, Dyl how fast were you driving? You shouldn't be home yet." He sounded angry and even a bit worried. But in true Dyllan sarcasm I replied, "Well sorry dad didn't know my led foot was a problem!" He hesitantly replied, "I'm sorry Dyl, I just had this bad feeling and I was worried. That's all. I love you."

All was forgiven. I was such a pushover. I still didn't speak for a second while I managed to take a deep breathe and centered myself. "It's fine babe. I just got lucky with mostly green lights and no traffic. I won't lie, we all know I speed a little bit." I answered with a giggle and heard a ragged breathe through the phone when he said, "I know beautiful girl. Just be careful. I'm going to go now. Mom made it home not long after you left and wants to visit with me. Goodnight sweet girl!" He sounded so sad. I quickly replied , "G'night my love. I'll see you tomorrow?" I heard the smile in his voice when he said,"Definitely." Then he hung up and there was silence.

I walked in the house to find mom reading one of her romance novels and smiled, wondering who she'd been dreaming about that tonight. Mom didn't date much. I asked her once, why and she said that she liked her life the way it was and why ruin it with an imperfect man when she could have had the one of her dreams every night in a book. I didn't get it, but I'd never had my heart ripped out of my chest like she had. Yeah my dad did a real number on her, but you would never know. She was the master of normalcy, but when she thought we were asleep at night and she was alone, I heard her sobs. I didn't quite understand that kind of pain. Yeah I was sad that my dad didn't want us, but he wasn't a good man. Mom was our everything. She did it all. She didn't need him.

I pulled myself out of my memory and said, "Well, hello mamasita! You are looking particularly gorgeous this evening." She stood from the couch and embraced me in a hug that only a mother could give. Swaying me back and forth, she said, "I almost didn't recognize you baby girl. I'm glad your home. Now tell me about what you've been doing. PG 13 please. No gory details Dyl!" I nodded being reminded of the days that I didn't like to share my thoughts with her and would tell her the most inappropriate things in an attempt to make her quit asking.

But mom just listened even though I knew she was only

A Minor Happy Ending

listening to stay close to me. At the time I hated her for it, but now I was grateful for it! "Well we ended up camping at Jade's house and he played a song he wrote for me. He wrote it a while ago, he loves me!" She smiled, but it was guarded, I knew she was holding back. I began to tell her the rest of the events of that evening. She listened to me when I told her about my talk with Nick and she got a kick out of me farting on Jace's lap. My face still heated up just thinking about it. She seemed genuinely pleased for me, but the cautious smile remained. She liked Jace, I could tell, but I didn't understand what had her so troubled. I ignored her expression not wanting to ruin this day with an argument, so I gave her hug and retreated to my room. As I drifted off to sleep, I thought of Jace and how lucky I was to find him. How I'd never felt that way before and I loved it.

I awoke to a chime and realized that I had a text message.

Jace: *you awake?*

Me: *well now I am, are you ok?*

Jace: *ya, I'm just missing having you here next to me. Was having trouble sleeping.*

Me: *miss you too babe. Call me and we can talk until you fall asleep.*

I placed my phone on vibrate and waited for the call. I waited five minutes and nothing. As I picked up my phone to text him and figure out what the problem was, my phone vibrated.

"Hey I didn't think you were going to call. Are you sure your okay?" I blurted, excited to hear from him. With a quiet chuckle he responded, "Ya, I'm fine. Like I said, I just miss you." He took a deep breathe and said, "Do I sound like a girl? Cause I feel like I'm acting like a girl." This made me giggle. How could that sexy man have any lack in confidence. He was the hottest thing I'd ever seen. "So, what do ya want to talk about baby? Music, movies, what schools we are going to this fall?" Then I heard faint snoring on the other end if the line. That was funny, I didn't remember him snoring before. I muttered, "Well that was quick!" Under my breath and listened to him rest. I listened to him breathe and drifted off to sleep.

When I awoke, the call had ended, but there was a text message awaiting me.
Jace: *if I can't have you with me that was the next best thing. Love you sugar. I'll see ya tonight.*

A Minor Happy Ending

Chapter 20

I had spent the morning doing laundry and cleaning for mom. She worked so hard and never complained, it was the least I could do. I placed my uniform on my bed and decided to turn on the TV to find an old chick flick to watch. About half way through the movie there was a knock on the door. I opened the door to find my two best friends. "What up chicas?" I said with enthusiasm as I encircled both of their necks and squeezed. After simultaneous hellos and returned squeezes we had a seat on the couch. "Ah shit Dyl, that movie again? How many times do you have to see that guy with a boom box over his head!" Jade said exuberantly. Max and I giggled, then Max spoke up, "Dyl may play the hard ass, but we all know she's just a sappy romantic at heart."
Nice Max Nice.
"Thanks for the support ladies" I murmured feigning annoyance. They laughed in return. That was why I loved

our friendship, it was easy. We could tell each other anything and it was ok. Max spoke up first, "So tell us how it's going with sex on a stick Harvey!" WOW, did that come from Max? I asked curiously, "Sex on a stick, huh?" Jade quickly jumped in, "Uh ya, I don't even like boys that much, but I'd let him do me once a day and twice on Sunday!" I couldn't help but guffaw at the comment my newly outed friend said. "Well let's just say the rumors are true. He is sex on a stick, but he is also sweet, funny, kind, goofy, and a bit protective of me, which I kind of like. It makes me feel safe." They both nodded knowing that I'd basically took care of myself since my dad left, so that my mom just had to worry about herself and Jenna. Not that mom didn't take care of me, but I grew up a little quicker than some. "Well, I'm glad your home because it's about time you hang out with your girls. Get ready, we are taking you to lunch, then we are hanging at the lake for a while" she said excitedly. "I've got to work tonight guys" I said sadly. She quickly replied,"Girl, you'll be back in plenty of time. Grab your suit, sunscreen and towel." I hopped up off of the couch with my marching orders and did as I was told, when I heard Jade call out, "And don't forget the sunscreen. I don't want to hear you whine for days about a sunburn!"

We climbed into Jade's yellow Mustang and opened the sunroof. It was abnormally warm for late spring, so no

A Minor Happy Ending

wonder they wanted to hit the lake for some fun today. "Hey, let's just hit a drive thru and eat at the lake." I said. "Sounds like a plan." Jade said as Max nodded in agreement.

When we arrived half of our senior class was already there splashing around or hanging out on the beach. We saw a few people we used to hang out with and chatted it up for a bit before picking our spot. We decided on a spot with partial shade and partial sun, so if I needed a break from the sun it could've been found easily.

I was normally a bit pale, but now my skin was kissed by the sun, my freckles were more prominent than they were in the winter months.

We stripped down to our suits and decided to lay out a bit before heading in the water. We spread out on the blankets, lay face down first and listened to the music playing over the loudspeaker. It wasn't bad today. They rotated the radio stations they used daily. It was a guess to what would be playing, it was like Russian Roulette with music. Jade still remembered the horror of showing up on Polka day! She told us she was waiting for people with lederhosen to come out and start dancing! She had a flare for the dramatic, but hell she was funny! Today's selection was the local pop music station, which played some music we enjoyed.

As I lay there, I began my people watching. A girl in a

bikini who kept repeatedly adjusting her boobs. A guy who played beach volleyball. A group of girls ogled the guy playing beach volleyball. So, out of curiosity I had to take a second look to see what the big deal was. I guess he was cute with curly blonde hair, tan athletic build with piercing blue eyes, and a sexy smile. Not as sexy as Jace's though, but not bad to look at. That was when Mr. Sexy's eyes landed on mine! Ah, shit! He caught me looking and shit he was walking over here! I quickly turned my head and pretended that I wasn't looking his way. He sauntered over to us, I saw the shadow before I heard his deep southern drawl, "Well freckles it's not nice to stare then play hard to get." "Well I'm sure your cheering section over there can help you with your ego boost cowboy, so ya might want to send your attentions that way" I quipped wanting to stop this before it started. Next thing I knew cowboy was lying next to me on the ground clutching his chest rolling back and forth writhing on the ground like he'd been shot. I jolted upward! What the hell was up with this guy? I had to admit this probably would've worked if I wasn't head over heels in love with Jace. He finally spoke up after his oscar worthy performance, "Well I'm pretty sure any confidence I have, has now been cast away by one freckled faced beauty." He said feigning sadness. He continued, "You could at least tell me your name since you just knocked me off my game." Shaking my head, I finally gave in to help

A Minor Happy Ending

end this conversation quickly, "I'm Dyllan, I'm with my two girlfriends here and I'm taken!" His eyes widened at my bluntness, then a determined smile displayed on his face. Max and Jade seemed to be enjoying our banter due to their muffled laughter, while their faces remained hidden in the blanket. "Well Dyllan, I'm gonna keep callin' ya freckles cause Dillon is my name too." He said with a smirk on his face. Well look at that, hmm? I couldn't flirt with the cowboy, I felt like I was betraying Jace, but there was no reason to be rude. I told him that I was taken. He spoke up bringing me out of my head, "Well freckles I'm sorry you're taken, but that doesn't tell me why you were staring my way?" He asked. "I people watch and I was wondering what that group of girls was staring at and it happened to be you." I took a deep breath and continued with my explanation "It's a game we play, we people watch and then make up stories about their lives. Totally bogus of course, but fun nonetheless." He nodded in understanding and said,"Let's play this game!" I quickly added, "As long as you know that you'd probably get a lot further with one of those other girls." He nodded and said, "Loud and clear freckles, but it's nice to have a new friend anyhow. Plus it's just a game, I can check in with my cheering section, that's what you called it right?" I nodded and laughed at his attempt to charm me. Ok I'd show him our game then dismiss him to his harem. "Ok cowboy, you first. Pick anyone you want." He picked a short brunette who had been splashing around in the water with her friends. She was plain, but pretty. Olive toned skin and a nice smile. He said,"She's cute right?" I nodded and he continued, "What you don't know she works for NASA training Monkeys." I asked "Oh yeah, train them to do what?" perking up my left brow. He closed his eyes, let his head fall back onto the towel, and let out a frustrated sigh and said, "How to read the food tubes so they can eat well-balanced meals?" Ah, that was terrible, poor guy! He was definitely outmatched here. I rolled my eyes and shook my head feigning disappointment and shouted, "That was weak, cowboy!" The girls and I joined him in laughter. Cowboy sat and played our game for a little. He was impressed by mine and Jade's mad skills for story-telling and finally said, "Ok freckles, I think I'm at a loss because you guys are finding easy targets. I get to pick your next victim!" I nodded and rolled my eyes at his poor sportsmanship. "Ok hmm? What poor sucker should I choose freckles?" He paused, pointed toward the parking lot and said, "That guy, the one in the black concert tee." My eyes followed his gaze and landed on the sexiest man I'd ever seen. Jace. My heart expanded, I was so excited to see him that I jumped up from my towel and rushed over to him with my arms wide. I felt his arms wrap around me swooping me up into his chest and holding on tight. I forgot all about our game and concentrated only on Jace. I was so excited, I blurted, "Oh baby I'm so happy you're here, I missed you like crazy! I didn't know you were coming!" He sat me down. He had a flaccid look on his face. His eyes were fixed and narrowed. No sweet grin appeared in his lips. No sign of the easy going nature I'd grown to love so much. "It was supposed to be a surprise and I am definitely surprised. Really, it looks like you were having plenty of fun without me. " He said in a cruel tone and stormed off. I stood there dumbfounded for a moment when anger filtered in and I thought out loud, "What the fuck was that?" Startled that I spoke my thoughts aloud, I looked back at my friends to find Smith nestled beside Max and Jade stared at me with concern in her eyes. I waved her off so that she didn't over dramatize what was going on. I understood he got jealous, but what the heck? There had to be something else going on and I was going to find out. I stalked off after him having to walk twice as fast just to catch up with him. I found him nestled up against a shade tree brooding and pouty. I decided to handle this with caution and try a little humor to lighten the mood. "Hey, how does a fish pee under water?" His eyes peered up at me and stared in my direction. Not exactly at me, but near me. I gave up on waiting for him to answer since he still felt like pouting and answered for him, "With his gill bladder!" Fake laughter ensued from my lips until a small smile appeared on his. I continued,"Ya know I heard that from my boyfriend. I was missing him like crazy while I was out with my friends, but I did enjoy my time with them. We even met a new friend who by the way totally knew that I have someone that I'm completely in love with and find to be the hottest piece of ass I've ever seen!" I sing songed. Then his smile grew and I felt a strong set of arms wrap around my waist pulling my body flush with his. He whispered "mine" in my ear like I didn't already know this. Our relationship was new and it wasn't like we started out on good terms. We both had some trust issues to work on. So, this time he got a pardon for his bad behavior. "Next time handsome, don't be so quick to jump to conclusions. I meant it when I said I love you. You are the only man I've ever said that to. That guy did have intentions, but I shot it down quickly. He sat with ALL THREE OF US" I annunciated "And played our people watching game too. Gotta say he kind of sucked at it!" That caused a more prominent smile and then he kissed me. A heated kiss with so much passion and love I felt like I melted into a puddle, but in pure Dyllan fashion, I couldn't keep my mouth shut. I broke away from his kiss and asked, "So was that all you were upset about or was there something else? I feel like I'm the only one speaking here baby?" Then his smile widened and he finally spoke, "Well who can get a word in when you are talking Sugar?" And all was well in the world

A Minor Happy Ending

again. I wrapped my arms around him again, pressed my lips against his, and felt the nice firm pressure. He caressed my lips with his and let his love for me flow through them. I'd never felt more adored and safe. He grabbed my hands and entwined our fingers and said, "This is the real thing, Sugar. I'll get past this jealousy thing I promise, but please give me time. All I want is you and the thought of someone trying to take you infuriates me to no end! I know you love me. No doubt in my head. Let's just enjoy our day. Smith called and said that Max wanted him to pick me up and meet you guys here at the lake. Some bonding time with the new boyfriend kind of thing. I blew something off, but since I get to see you it is totally worth it. Plus being able to stare at you in a bikini is a big motivator!" He chuckled acting like nothing happened. I was glad he already let it go, but there was something still plaguing him a little. I could feel it, but I wouldn't press him today. Maybe it was because his parents were in town and he didn't want to deal with them. I'd ask later. For now I just wanted to be with him.

We walked hand in hand back to our blanket and joined our friends. Cowboy stuck around and flirted with Jade since he officially saw that I was taken. Boy was he ever barking up the wrong tree, but I was sure it helped Jade pass the time. She didn't need to feel like the fifth wheel. Jace even struck up a conversation with Cowboy about music. Cowboy was actually pretty musically intellectual. We spent the rest of the afternoon relaxing on the beach until I had to leave for work. Jace drove me home in Smiths car. He rode with Max and Jade in the Mustang. Our kiss lasted a small forever with hands and mouths roaming everywhere. The pull was so strong sometimes. I dragged myself away, he told me that the gang would be stopping by The Diner to see me. Excited to hear the news, I smiled and blew him a kiss before I got ready for work.

Chapter 21

About two hours in, The Diner was swamped even for a Saturday night. I hadn't completed any of my side work, yet and my tables had been full. We were generally busier in the summer, because kids were out of school and teenagers didn't want to go home. Plus, there wasn't much else to do here after midnight that wouldn't get you into trouble. Our crowd tonight had consisted mostly of the younger variety and of course the people that just left the bar. Six more hours to go, but I'd already made sixty two dollars. That was pretty good, even for a Saturday night. I took a mini break in the back and swallowed a pop, when Barb told me that I was just seated some new customers. I placed a smile on my face even though the day in the sun wore me out. Max and Jade called it my fake smile and my fake voice accompanied it.

I walked up not entirely paying attention to the table when I walked up and said, "Welcome to The Diner?

What can I get for ya?" with the brightest smile I could muster. I looked up to find my friends smiling back at me and showing all of their teeth. Jace was there with an amused smile on his face and Smith had his eyes on Max. Oh yeah and Cam sat between Jade and Jace with a devilish grin on her face. She looked like the cat that ate the canary. I wondered what she had done now. I looked at Jace and he stared back at me adoringly, so I relaxed a little. Whatever it was, she wouldn't win. I felt a little triumphant when I noticed Nick wasn't with her. I'd be the better person for now. Jace was the first to speak up, "Wow, sugar they were right you do have a fake voice when you are working." he said with a chuckle. I rolled my eyes and quickly quipped "See, this is my nice voice and it's only reserved for people who actually deserve it." His eyes widened in surprise. He must've been waiting for me to blush, but he still had a lot to learn about me. Then his expression changed as the rest of the crew hassled him about my remark. He looked amused, but at the same time uncertain. So, I leaned down and with my warm breathe I spoke into his ear for only him to hear. "Good thing that's the only thing that I have to fake." I watched him adjust himself in the seat, it just turned me on knowing that just the feel of my breathe and a few sexy words and I got him. He was all mine. Then he turned to me with eyes so dark that the blue was almost gone and said, "I will be here when you get off and then you will come home with me and I will get you off again and again." Hot damn! I was at work, wet and wanting Jace. Then it dawned on me that he said home with him and I asked aloud, "Aren't your parents home? I'm sure your mom doesn't want me to sleep over." He shook his head and said, "She had an unexpected meeting and had to leave and dad never made it home. They'll be gone four more days then come home for two. So does that mean I can have my girl with me for the next four days?" I could cut the sexual tension with a knife! I needed him on me, around me, and in me and preferably multiple times! It took all my willpower not to take him out back, strip him bare and have him take me up against the wall until we both can no longer stand. That scene replayed in my head repeatedly when I was rudely interrupted by bitch face. "Can I order or what I'm starving?" she said with venom disguised as sarcasm in her tone. That girl was far from starving. She could afford to wait a bit. But yet again, bigger person! Be the bigger person Dyllan. I placed my smile back on my face, I over exaggerated my happy voice and asked, "Well sure Cam, what can I get for ya?" Ya it was a bit condescending, but sometimes I couldn't help myself. I was trying though. She barked out her order like the dog she was and smiled, showing me all her dingy teeth. I finished writing down their orders and placed them in the system. I filled their drinks and checked on my other customers while waiting for their food to come up. My eyes periodically drifted over to my friends and Jace met my gaze. The heat in his stare was mesmerizing. Cam noticed and dragged his face from mine asking him a question. He seemed annoyed, but like you would be with your baby sister. He didn't appear to have any feelings other than platonic toward her. Thank God! My buzzer went off letting me know that their food was ready, I grabbed their food and asked if they needed anything else. It seemed that everyone was happy at the moment so I asked another waitress, Becca to watch my tables so I could take a ten minute break. My feet were sore. I hid in the back dining room we used for private parties instead of the break room that most of the staff resided for their break times, since I mostly kept to myself. I climbed into one of the large booths and took off my shoes.

    I rested my eyes for a moment, just breathing and humming my song in my head. It was so amazing that I had my own song. I reveled in my happiness for about two minutes when a knock sounded on the door and Becca peeked her head in. "Yep, just where I thought she'd be!" She said in her sugary sweet tone. She opened the door wider and there he was, My Jace. He winked and smiled, thanking her for her help. She blushed from her chest to her ears and giggled like a school girl. Oh my baby's charm

A Minor Happy Ending

would get him into trouble one day. But not today since he used it to see me. He walked in casually until she closed the door then his steps were more determined as I stood and he made his way toward me. His arms quickly wrapped around my waist, lifted me and my legs encircled around his tight frame. Next thing I knew, I was on the table top, he was kissing me with more passion causing all the warmth to pool between my legs and small moans escaped my throat. "Ah, Sugar when you moan my pants become way too tight. I want you Dyl. I don't know if I can wait until later. I need to know what I still do to you sugar." His hands traveled between my legs, I knew that he felt the warmth, while nibbling and trailing kisses down my neck and shoulders. I gasped and he answered with a moan of his own, wanting him to touch me more. "No noise Dyllan, I'm going to make you feel good baby, but no noise. Those are only for me. I don't share what's mine." Loving what his controlling nature was doing to my body, I shuddered . He lifted up my long black skirt, pressed his palm against me adding the perfect pressure in circular motions. He pressed his lips so hard against mine that our teeth smacked into one another. Until I could no longer handle the pressure building within my body, I fell apart all over the table. When I came back to earth, his crooked grin was present. He looked pleased with himself. Well hell I was definitely pleased with him. He just gave me an amazing orgasm in less than a couple minutes. He kissed me one last time and said, "Just a preview for later, sugar." He lifted his hand and inhaled deeply. If it was anyone else, I would've been grossed out, but knowing he loved the smell of me was a turn on. I spoke up, "You can't go out there like that." I said pointing to his jeans with a very noticeable bulge. I'd never get him home. The girls in this place would go into heat and I'd have to get a cattle prod to get him out. He chuckled and said, "I'll go to the restroom and think of my grandma skiing naked. Yep that should work just fine!" He chuckled and I reciprocated. "Oh and Sugar, will you come home with me for a few days? Nothing would make me happier." he said sweetly. I nodded and sighed at my sexy man. Ya know that saying, I hate to see ya go, but love to watch you leave! I was pretty sure that they were talking about Jace. That man's backside was delicious! And all mine!

After I went to the restroom to regain my composure, I checked on my tables to see if they needed anything, saving my friends table for last. A couple of refills later, the crew prepared to leave and Cam took Jace's arm. Probably just to annoy me, but he shook her off and told them, "Dyl gets off in an hour, I'm just going to hang out here and take her home, okay?" It wasn't really a question, but Cam retorted, "But you haven't been over in weeks, I miss my friend. We are just going to watch some movies, Dyllan can

A Minor Happy Ending

come over after work is she wants" sounding whiney. He separated their arms making distance between him and Cam and said, "I'd rather be here with her." He said forcefully making his intentions known. Maybe he could see what she was doing. Maybe I wasn't jumping to conclusions after all. Everyone said their goodbyes and I waved at most of them. I refilled Jace's drink and attended to my other customers. In the meantime I attempted to complete my side work so I could leave as soon as we closed. When my side work was done, all I had were two tables, Jace and one with a couple who were all over each other. It was twenty minutes before I could leave and I decided to chat with my man since all of my work was done. I walked over to find three paper napkin roses sitting on the table and asked Jace what he was doing. He said that Smith showed him how to make them, he felt that after our tryst in the back room, it was ungentlemanly of him not to bring flowers. I loved him more every day. When it was time to go, we jumped in my car with my napkin bouquet in hand. I allowed him to drive while I texted mom our plans, so that she didn't worry. She worried enough. She texted me back the typical thanks and to be careful, before I knew it we were there. The air felt thicker than normal tonight, like there was something brewing, but I wasn't sure what. Jace had something hidden behind those blue eyes I loved so much, but I'd wait. He'd tell me when he was ready. I trusted him. We went inside and the heaviness evaporated when we entered our sacred little bubble. He slowly snaked his arms around me and whispered, "Dyllan all I want is you here with me. I don't care if we're poor or rich. One kid or ten. I don't care as long as you are with me. I've felt more love in the couple of weeks we've been together than in my whole life. I need you to know that okay?" At the beginning of that statement my heart was swooning, but near the end I was so confused. I wasn't sure why I would need to know that. Questioning looks must've masked my features when he continued,"Don't worry Dyl, everything is fine. I need to move out of the house. Cam said that I can stay with her and that's where I will be living for a while. I've got a construction job, getting paid under the table for the rest of the summer. I know you and Cam don't get along very well, but my options are limited." My stomach clenched and I felt like I was going to vomit. Cam? Why her? I was stunned, staring at the love me my life waiting for the punch line, but it never came. He patiently waited for my response, when he realized that I didn't have one, he came closer and placed a loose strand of my hair behind my ear. He looked into my eyes that have recently filled with unwanted tears and whispered, "You have nothing to worry about Dyllan. I'm not Nick and the only person I see is you." Normally that would've calmed me down and

A Minor Happy Ending

melted my insides, but the longer I listened to him talk, the angrier I got. I felt the festering heat of anger build until I could no longer hold it in and I burst, "Ya you're right, you're no Nick! Nick would've at least consulted with me first before deciding to move in with someone who totally hates my guts and tries to steal everything that is mine. She waits until I'm at my most vulnerable and pounces, but noooooo need to worry Dyl. Not at all. Ya know what, why wait for Cam to break us up? Later!" I ran out his front door and raced to the Century, but I didn't get very far because he was right on my tail. I opened the door of the Century and a force on the door caused it to close. He looked bigger than normal, his eyes on fire, his chest heaving and his hands clenched at his sides. Then in a venomous whisper he said, "You are not leaving me Dyl. Get your ass back into the house so we can talk about this like adults, now," as he leaned in closer to me so I felt his breath on my neck. But I mustered my strength and with equal venom asked, "Why the fuck should I? You've made your decision already and obviously you don't give a fuck what my opinion is?" Then he erupted, "Did you not fucking listen Dyllan, I have no other choice. I have to move in with Cam or I have to leave. My parents and I had a fight and they are on their way home now. If I move in with Cam I stay with you. If I don't I'll have to leave." He sounded so defeated, my heart broke for him. I couldn't believe his parents expected him to move the summer before college. I couldn't help but think what the hurry was about? I stared up at him and waited. Not sure what to say, so I grabbed his hand and allowed him to lead me back into the house. When we got inside, he wrapped me into his strong embrace, just holding and breathing each other in. He pulled away from me and explained that when he made enough money that he wanted to get his own place and for me to eventually move in. Surprisingly that didn't remotely scare me. What scared me was Cam trying to get her nasty claws into my man. He was still giving me vague details, but I pushed for more answers. I wasn't afraid to piss him off anymore. This was my life too and I had a right to know why it was changing. "Jace, these vague answers are not cutting it. Why would your parents want you to move when college starts in 3 months? Did they already sell the house? Tell me!" At first he looked confused, then frustrated, then he nodded and said, "I have to leave before they get home. I won't have a choice when they get here. I'm moving into Cam's in three days." Sounding even more defeated than before and continued, "I even got a new number so they wouldn't be able to find me okay? Give me your phone, Dyl." I handed him my phone and watched him replace his old number with his new one and explained, "It's prepaid. So? Are we okay now? Will you take me to Cam's? I'm leaving my car here

A Minor Happy Ending

too?" I looked at him dumbfounded, not quite sure what to say to all of this and prayed that this wasn't the beginning of the end for us. "Fine, I'll take you, but you have to give me time to deal with this." I said with more heat than intended. The next thing I knew I was pressed up against the front door with my legs around his waist. At first he was breathing me in, smelling my neck and began trailing kisses up my neck, behind my ear where he began to taste me. He pulled back to stare at me asking my permission without words and I nodded. In one grand gesture, he stood me pulled my shorts and undies off in one swoop. Did the same thing to his clothes, slowly applying the condom on my favorite part of his anatomy, then in an instant he lifted me and entered me slowly. I felt every glorious inch of him enter and exit my body bringing me closer to ecstasy. He never took his eyes off of mine for a second, when I was about to fall over the edge he commanded,"Don't close your eyes Dyl. Stay with me the entire time. I want to see you when you come. I want your beauty imprinted on my mind like that always, Dyl. Always." With those words I fell apart staring into the blue eyes of the man that had tamed me for only him. Who showed his love for me through his words and through his eyes. Who wrote me a beautiful song, telling me he loved me. On my way down from my orgasm I felt and saw his need, I held on tight to find the most glorious feeling as he spiraled out of control.

    Tears welled in my eyes, I saw the concern on his face as I spoke, "I just love you so much Jace. The thought of her doing something to make you leave me hurts so much." He replied with an equal amount of emotion, "Sugar, the only way I'd leave you, is if I was forced to." And I believed him.

A Minor Happy Ending

Chapter 22

3 days later

We loaded some boxes and a couple of suitcases in the Century and I drove him to Cams. We pulled into Cam's drive and she had another party going on tonight. The usual people were there, I had to come to terms that this was my life for the next few months.

Jade and Max were there. Smith must've been busy, since I didn't see him. I walked up onto the porch and hugged my girls enthusiastically. They hugged me back with fervor whispering reassurances in my ears. I loved how my girls could just read me and knew exactly what to say. Cam must've told them what was going on. I was sure she had that smug grin plastered on her face playing it off like she was being a great friend. She had that act down to a science. I'd been avoiding her since the night I caught her with Nick. It was hard to admit it, but it still hurt, now I was stuck with her for the next few months. I mustered up enough courage to find Jace since he darted in ahead of me. I gave my friends one last look as I saw Jade pass a bottle of some sort of alcohol to Max. I intercepted it on the pass and took two large gulps of the tart substance. A little liquid courage I guess, I threw a bit of caution to the wind. I didn't normally drink too often, I usually could find enough fun on my own without creating the unhealthy kind, but I was only young once. Right?

Max giggled and chanted "CHUG CHUG CHUG!" as Jade laughed and joined in. The next thing I knew the whole party was watching me drown my sorrows in the bottle. But I didn't feel sorrowful, I felt good, great even. I forgot all about Cam and about Jace moving in here. It was amazing not worrying for five minutes. I decided not to go find Jace yet and just enjoy the party instead. I hung out on the porch with my girls singing, dancing and drinking. Then of course, I had to pee! Always! I swear my bladder was the size of a pea. I notified the girls that I'd make a swift return and headed inside, Max quickly ran up behind me and joined me. Linking arms we continued to talk about nonsense as we hurried to Cam's small bathroom. I rushed to the toilet and peed first, not feeling too bad that I just took privileges, but she knew I had a tiny bladder. Then as I washed my hands, I waited for her to pee while we chatted about what'd been going on with us. She told

A Minor Happy Ending

me how well she and Smith were getting along, I told her how in love I was with Jace and she said, "It's pretty obvious to everyone that he believes the sun rises and sets on you, Dyl." I slowly replied,"It does on him too." I said honestly and her eyes widened, but turned gentle. "Never thought I'd see the day you were whipped! It's a nice look for ya." she said happily. I knew she loved me. I loved her in return, we drunkenly embraced and not so stealthy left the bathroom on tip toes for the people watching a movie in the living room. Then I saw Jace come out of Cam's room looking flustered as slammed the door. I watched him run his fingers through his short blonde hair and sighed. He didn't look happy, I didn't like where he came from. The jealous part of me was winning right now, as I felt my face turn red and my eyes narrowed when his gaze met mine. His eyes widened for a moment, then realization crept in to his expression. He started charging my way as I grabbed Max's arm and led her to the porch. I just didn't want to fucking hear it right now. We'd been here what an hour and already she'd dug her claws into him. Fuck what was I thinking. I was doing just fine not falling in love with anyone. Max saw my expression and whispered, "Stay calm Dyl, ya don't know what happened. I doubt it's what you think and you just told me yourself that you guys are in love." Damn it Max couldn't just let me be mad for two seconds before trying to talk sense into me! Ugh! We were almost to the bench out front, when Max sat and I was all of a sudden being dragged by my arm to my car. "Fuck Dyl, are you drunk?" he said loudly. "Why yes Mr. Can't keep his dick in his pants I am, but at least I'm not fucking a nasty troll behind my girlfriend's back!" I said with venom. He jolted back like I'd just slapped him. "Thanks for having so much faith in me Dyl, faith in us!" He paused then reluctantly continued, "I was leaving a message for my parents letting them know that I wasn't coming home. Then Cam walked in stripping with some guy. I asked her to leave since I was on the phone. She told me that this was her house and I could either stay and watch or get the fuck out!" My blood boiled after that statement. Stay and watch huh? That was how she was planning on getting to him. By being slutty! Well hopefully she realized slutty was not sexy! My man preferred sexy. My emotions calmed a little, I relaxed my shoulders and touched his firm chest. My hands traveled up his chest and down his arms. In a seductive whisper I stated, "When everyone is gone, I want to christen every part of this house!" Slowly his crooked grin was in place and his hard body was against mine as well as the hardness between his legs when he said, "Sugar, you can't do this to me. I'm seriously tenting my pants right now. So, now your getting punished! You must stand here with me telling me the most putrid things to make my hard on go away." "Or what?" I quickly added. "Or this"

A Minor Happy Ending

and he began to tickle me again knowing that my tiny bladder caused terrible consequences even though I just went. I doubled over in laughter and begged to be let go and he complied. He just held me close and danced with me for a few songs when Jade and Max asked to cut in. Max grabbed me and Jade grabbed Jace. We spent the rest of the evening enjoying each other's company.

The first full day at Cams apartment, we didn't see too much of her. She went to bed so late that she slept most of the day away. Then she had to work, so Jace and I had the whole apartment to ourselves and christened a few rooms of the house. I refused to go into Cams room, didn't know what kind of diseases a person could get in there, but the kitchen, living room and bathroom. CHECK, CHECK, AND CHECK! Maybe these next few months wouldn't be so bad. "Dyl, white or wheat?" he asked. "Wheat, duh?" I replied gingerly awaiting this famous french toast he kept bragging about. I feigned indifference, but I was actually excited to see more of his talents since he had so many. Seriously the guy should suck at something, but I was willing to wait to find out.

Chapter 23

Five months later.

These past few months practically living at Cam's had been a whirlwind of wild parties, new friends, and love. Obsessive, heated, passionate love. Jace had made it his mission to keep our bubble intact. When he looked at me, it was like there was no one else in the room. He made it obvious to everyone that he had eyes for me alone. Jade and Max were frequent visitors to Cam's apartment. Max and Jace became very close and had a sibling like bond which made me happy. Jade appeared skeptical of Jace, but shown no ill will towards him. She kept her thoughts to herself, but I saw it.

Basically when Jace moved in with Cam, so did I. She still made snide remarks about me owing rent too. Jace defended me by telling her that he already payed more than his share and that should've made up for mine.

A Minor Happy Ending

At times he became distant usually when we were away from Cam's. It worried me some, because between school, work and family, I was afraid we would either become hermits or fall apart. The only interaction we had with other people were at Cams and when I wanted to go out he seemed nervous. It had only happened a few times, but I noticed him wringing his hands and his eyes darting around. I thought maybe his parents might've been looking for him and he was afraid to leave me. I needed to somehow get him to confess and to help him figure out a way to fix their relationship. I'd tried to talk with him about contacting them a few times, he shut down the conversation quickly stating that they didn't care about him while he was growing up so they wouldn't care now. I wouldn't let his hermit ass keep me from enjoying my youth, so when Max asked me to go dancing tonight I was quick to agree. I stopped by Cam's on my way home from school to see if Jace made it home from work and to let him know my plans. Partially because I wanted to let him know my plans, partially because I wanted to coax him out of the house. He wouldn't have been able to stand the thought of me dancing at Club 43 without him. I knocked while I was opening the door to find the living room empty and yelled "Hello?" And I'm greeted with Jace wearing only a towel and that crooked smile. Wow, the things that smile did to me. "Hi baby." I said seductively trying to stir things in him. "Hello to you too Sugar. How was school?" as he wrapped his strong arms around me and squeezed, sniffing my neck and I shivered at his nearness. I replied, "Good. I learned the function of the digestive system today." He perked an eyebrow and replied,"That sounds interesting enough." Nodding I sarcastically sing-song, "Nah, just a fancy way of explaining the process of pooping." He rolled his eyes and shook his head and said," What am I going to do with you Dyl?" I giggled as he slapped my butt. That was when I decided to break the news regarding my night out. "Hey babe, Max invited me out to Club 43 with her tonight, so I figured I'd come see you tonight before I went out with her." I sprouted out in one breath. His body became rigid and he was holding his breath, when he replied, "Oh what's the special occasion? Smith know about this?" he asked while stepping back and rubbing his hands through his hair. As innocently as I could muster I said, "Well you could always come with us if ya want?" As I walked up to him and ran my hands up his chest, his eyes lit up and he snaked his arms around my waste and murmured in my ear, "I can think of so many better things to do with my time." As he began to let his hands roam. They slid up my back and glided down my arms. The slithered around my waste and landed on my ass cupping the plumpness. He began to knead the tissue

A Minor Happy Ending

as he trailed kisses down my neck causing my body to shiver. "Ya cold Sugar?" He said in a smolderingly smug tone which brought me out of my stupor.

"Yep, just cooled right off!" I said as I backed up and shook my index finger at him. "No way bucko! You are not changing my mind with lovin! Not this time. Baby, I want to go out." I whined, "We barely ever go out anymore. You can't keep me cooped up forever." He looked defeated and exhaled. He ran those big strong hands through his hair and stepped forward resting his forehead onto mine. He said, "Ok Sugar, you win. We will go dancing."

Triumphantly I lifted my arms and jumped up and down like Rocky. I asked, "You mean you are going too? You don't have to if you don't want to," in a pouty tone. "Yes I'm going. If I can't run my hands all over you here then I'll have to do it there. I can't have all those men staring at my girl while I'm sitting on my ass. Besides, I'm sure Smith will want to go too and he could use some company." he explained. I felt my lips twitch and musically stated, "Awe baby, are you a jelly fish?" His face turned a few shades of red and he shook his head. When he looked into my eyes it was almost predatory when he whispered, "Mine".

Yep that had got to be my favorite words he said. It caused my brain to stop working, my body to take control, but I was going to stand my ground.

Will power please work! Please!

I forced myself away from him and sighed. I relaxed my shoulders and said, "Well, I'll go home and get ready then." He grabbed my arm as I turned to walk away, slammed my body into his and I felt his towel fall.

Damn that man could cause my brain to completely shut down. Then he said, "We have some time Sugar. I want the smell of me all over you while we are out tonight. There is nothing sexier than when you smell like me." I felt the tightening in my belly and wetness between my legs.

Oh fuck it!

I jumped up and wrapped my legs around his waist as he propped me on the kitchen island and hurriedly ripped my undies off, lifted my skirt until it flew over my head. My shirt and bra followed quickly. There was no slow cherishing movements. This was pure need. The need to show me that I was his.

The need to feel me close to him.

The need to feel me love him.

I do. I love him.

 He entered me slowly at first until his need grew, then his movements became jerky and wild. He reached between us to play with my swollen clit causing my entire body to fall apart! A few more hard thrusts later and he joined me with his own release.

"The best way to mark your territory ever!" I announced causing that shy chuckle and crooked smile that I had grown to love so much. " I love you Sugar."

"And I love you"

"Just so you know, I plan on being your husband one day."

Huh? Weird? Doesn't freak me out?

It actually felt good. It felt good that he wanted a future with me. It felt good that even though we'd only been together a short time, he was so sure of me.

I didn't know if I was that sure of myself.

I must've been in my head a bit too long when his hand waved in front of my face and he said with a small frown "Sorry Dyl, probably too soon."

"No, don't be sorry. I was just thinking how that didn't freak me out like it would've before. I just kept thinking how good that sounds."

"I'm not saying we do it tomorrow Dyl, but will you? Will you wake up next to me for the next fifty years? Will you have my babies and help me chase them around the yard? Will you help me count my wrinkles and give the grand kids extra candy? I want that life Dyl. I want that life with you. So, what do you think Dyllan. Will you marry me? It'll be a little ways away until I can afford to give you everything you deserve, but will you only be mine?"

"Baby, I've always been yours. And YES!" I shouted loudly. I knew it was crazy and we just graduated, but we didn't have to do it tomorrow. The look of awe on his face was amazing, he'd never looked more beautiful. The child like wonder was in his eyes when he looked at me. It was somewhat intimidating at times, but man it felt so good. He was meant for me and I for him.

I waited for Jace to dress and we walked hand in hand to the Century. I let him drive, happily taking the passenger seat. I watched him as he drove. The easy way he moved his hands, the way he tilted his head to the left trying to catch the breeze from the open window, and the way his shoulders rested back onto the seat showing complete ease was beautiful. He was so beautiful and mine. I still was having some trouble wrapping my head around his proposal. It kind of came out of left field, but it was the best surprise. Lackadaisically I twirled my hair and stared off in his direction, but not really focusing on anything in particular. I tended to do that when in deep thought. The vision of him blurred as I stared at the scenery go by and think about how these last six months together had flown by. It seemed like yesterday that I was sneaking glimpses of his crooked smile, smelling him when he leaned a little too close to me. I'd never been with anyone this long before or even wanted to. They were always gone by now, but I realized as I thought this that I never wanted him gone. Never! He'd become such a part of me that I wasn't sure what my life would've been without him. I couldn't believe how sappy I was sounding, but at the same time. I didn't give a shit. I knew I made the right decision! He was my heart!

My home!

"Dyl? Are you daydreaming again or do I have a huge booger?" he said jovially, waving his hand in front of my face attempting to bring me out of my haze. I nodded.

"Is it a gooooood dream?" He continued as he wiggled his eyebrows up and down. I shook my head and feigned disappointment and quickly retorted,

"Yep, I was dreaming of those blue eyes of yours!" He smiled and nodded. "That sexy crooked smile!" I said and his smile began to grow showing pearly white teeth. "And we can't forget my favorite part, babe." He looked at me with pride on his face. I knew he thought I was going to talk about his man parts! Gosh, even my Jace couldn't get over his man parts. It must've been a guy thing. I continued further, "and your big, no that doesn't do it justice, your huge..." I could tell he was on the edge of his seat waiting for the ultimate compliment.

"Ego!" His gorgeous blue eyes widened in surprise and an ornery smile displayed. He jutted his nose towards the ceiling and huffed in feign disgust. He replied with a devilish smile on his face as we pulled into my driveway, "Ego, huh? Well well well!" Something was about to happen and I wasn't quite sure what he had up his sleeve, but I would be keeping my eye on him. I reached for the door and he was quick to match my actions. I ran for the front porch to evade the retaliation for my smart ass comment, but I forgot that I couldn't run and I failed at my half brained attempt to out-run someone who was in better shape than me. He caught me quickly by the waist and tackled me to the ground. His hands reached up and began to assault each muscle that rested between my ribs. I was in a fit of giggles to the point that I began snorting at fairly loud decibels. As my face turned many shades of red and embarrassment invaded my brain, I continued my best Porky pig impression without fail. Sometimes I honestly wondered why he found me so attractive, but I was glad he did. When I could no longer take it, I cried out "Ok. Ok. Ok. Stop. Please. You're going to make me pee." A low chuckle erupted from his chest and he replied, "Tempting? Hmm? Should I or shouldn't I?" All of a sudden things got serious. I retorted, "Don't even think about it babe. I really can't take anymore." His hands reached out as if he was going for the kill, but then stopped. He reached down and wiped away a stray hair and placed it tenderly behind my ear. Our eyes locked and his blue eyes memorized me in a daze that I didn't want to leave. He began humming my song and I closed my eyes. We just lay in the grass like this for a little while and enjoyed each other. It was just easy.

When we heard a loud shriek and pattering footsteps, we

A Minor Happy Ending

jolted to see what happened and found Jenna running in our direction full speed yelling, " Dylan! Jace!" with the excitement usually saved for Christmas morning, maybe I'd been away for a little longer than I realized. Jace smiled as his gaze left mine, focused on his biggest fan and sincerely said, "Hello pretty girl." Her whole face lit up and a radiant smile adorned her beautiful freckled face. Her checks began to redden as her face heated up from the blush. She looked in awe at the beautiful man that I called mine and twisted her hands as he had risen to greet her. "Hi Jace." she replied softly and shyly asked, "and what are you doing to my sister?"

Now the blush grew up his cheeks and then a spark entered his eyes and he replied rather coyly,

"Well, pretty girl your sister had a bug in her eye and I was staring in there to see if I could find it. Then I'm pretty sure that she cast some sort of crazy spell on me, cuz all of a sudden I couldn't remember what happened just a few minutes ago. Have you noticed any weird activity going on with her lately?"

She giggled her sweet little belly laugh. I had hoped she never lost that. Most people did though. It was sad. It was an honest laugh. It was one that could never have been mistaken as fake and was the most contagious. Her laugh was so infectious that usually half of the room giggled along with her. But her wit usually shocked people.

"Other than spending every day with you? Nah." She said sarcastically.

Yep that was my little sis. Smart ass extraordinaire. Took after me! So proud. So proud.

Jace shook his head and laughed. He brushed off his pants and offered his hand to me when he said, "That is rather odd isn't it pretty girl? Now who would want to do such a thing? Geesh, she must be really screwed up to hang out with the likes of me, but I've got to tell ya. I think she secretly loves it! She may not admit it now, but I'm pretty sure that she does."

Jenna nodded and quickly added, "Well I do too!" Then Jace grabbed Jenna by the arms and threw her over his shoulder. She squealed as we all headed into the house, Jenna was giggling the entire way.

    As I showered and readied myself for our night out with friends, Jace entertained Jenna and mom with what I could only assume were his silly jokes from all of the laughter that I was hearing from the other room. He could've charmed his way through anything.

    I decided on a pale pink ruffled tank top and skinny jeans that my ass filled out entirely. Good thing it wasn't any bigger or skinny jeans would not be an option. I let my strawberry blonde hair air dry into soft waves. It was getting longer so it hung a bit past my shoulders now. My skin had a sun kissed glow, but my freckles were more

A Minor Happy Ending

prominent due to the sun. Jace said he thought that they were cute, but I'd never really been a big fan of them. Adding a little mascara and pink gloss to my lips, I was ready to go.

As I made my way into the living room to made my grand entrance, I overheard Jace's voice. "I honestly do, Mrs. Prescott. I can't imagine what life would be like without her. I promise I will never hurt Dyl. She's why I wake up and take that first breathe every day." I heard higher pitched mumbles, not able to make out the words, but the tone was serious, yet comforting. Knowing that my mom in her subtle way was giving him her version of a smack down, I entered the room gesturing grandly with my hand and announcing, "Ta-Da!" All eyes were on me. My mom and Jenna smiled complimenting me on my outfit. Jace's eyes darkened and I knew what he was thinking. His lust filled gaze caused my heart to quicken and I knew we were probably staring at each other longer than we should've been.

I brought myself out of my stupor to make sure I didn't embarrass myself in front of my mother and said, "Ya ready babe?" He nodded and stood, grabbing my hand and leading me toward the door. We waved and voiced our love and good-byes to my family on our way to pick up Max and meet the crew.

Chapter 24

    Club 43 was the busiest I'd seen. People crammed inside for each group that left, another group entered. We were lucky to only have to wait a short time. It was so busy, the police were patrolling the streets surrounding the club to play crowd control and possibly to catch any DUI activity. Smith offered to be the DD and of course Max was excited about that. She told me once that when her inhibitions were lowered and his weren't the sex was amazing. She told me she didn't feel sexy, but alcohol brought her out of her shell, hopefully one day she'd realize that she was beautiful, smart and sexy all on her own.

Shit, if I was a dude or into girls, I'd totally do her! Hopefully, Smith recognized what he had in his grasp. I watched as his hand landed on the small of her back leading her into the club showing everyone that she was his. Jace and I followed with our fingers intertwined.

A Minor Happy Ending

A proud smile appeared on his face as he released my hand and wrapped his arm around my waist holding me near. His way of letting the whole club know that I was his and he was mine.

Wilma Picklesimer and Anita Holder were out in full force tonight. We danced and sang along with the music, showing no care in the world. Max was burning up the dance floor and I tried to keep up with her. Jace and Smith sat at a nearby table nursing a couple of sodas, while babysitting our girly drinks as they called them.

One of my favorite songs played, I began to slowly rotate my hips to match the rhythm of the music. Max was beside me matching my movements and moving closer to me. We began dancing together and a wicked smile displayed on her face, knowing that the guys were watching us. She began to let her hands roam on my hips and thighs as she lowered herself and pressed her body against mine. I snuck a peek at our table and saw a pair of lustful gazes. Wow, it really was that easy wasn't it?

Both men's gazes lingered on where our bodies were grinding together, I saw my man adjust himself knowing what kind of effect that I was having on him. Smiths reaction surprised me, because he almost looked like he was about to jump out of his chair. Smith was more of subdued, but right now he looked like a caged animal ready to pounce. I stifled a giggle not wanting to be obvious with my success. His eyes were only for Max, he saw right through me, but that was ok, because I had my own man to pounce on me. I returned my stare in his direction when I saw his expression change, then Max and I were surrounded by two large chests. Large arms attempted to slither around my waist, but I quickly guided them away from me and shook my index finger back and forth at the big gorilla as a warning. He stepped back, but continued to dance near me. I chanced a glance at the table to find Smith and Jace gone.

I turned back to gorilla man to find him and Jace nose to nose. I grabbed Jace by the arm and gestured for us to leave. Jace was almost immovable, until I pinched the inside of his arm causing him to cringe and to come out of his temporary psychosis. I waved good bye to gorilla man, with a smarmy smile he returned the wave and shrugged. Watching Max tug Smith away through the front doors, I relaxed and followed. By the time we reached the exit, we found the happy couple lip locked with hands roaming and smacking sounds. I started to chuckle seeing the reaction Max had to Smith's jealousy and turned to enjoy the moment with Jace to find that his reaction remained the same as it was inside. Taken back by his reaction I dropped his hand and stormed off to the car. Mirroring my attitude. Jace was on my heels, I could feel the tension radiating off

A Minor Happy Ending

of his body. As I reached for the door handle, my hand was forced away and calloused fingers held it like a vice, when he erupted,"And what the fuck was that Dyl?" Shocked by the blame I was receiving I replied with venom, "It's not my fault some douchetard didn't take no for an answer!" He stared at me for a moment not quite sure what he was thinking. This moment seemed to last forever when he finally spoke, but not before that crooked smile appeared, "Douchetard?" As he erupted into laughter. I figured that I'd play more into his amusement, "Ya douchetard! Ya got a problem with that?" He raised his hands in surrender and shook his head while continuing to laugh. "Sugar, maybe you aren't as sweet as I originally thought." he said laughing. "Douchetard. I'm gonna use that one. I like it." The mood was lighter, but I was still mad that he couldn't see that I didn't do anything wrong. I took his hands off of me. This jealousy thing had to stop. If he still couldn't trust me then I didn't know if he ever would. Angrily I replied, "Glad I could do something right for you tonight Mr. Harvey," as I turned around and grabbed for the door again only to be stopped by those quick calloused hands. One of those beautiful hands cupped my chin causing me to turn my entire body to face him. He looked me in the eyes and rested his forehead to mine. After a few breathes he whispered, "I'm sorry Sugar. I just love you so much." I whispered back, "I love you too babe, you're going to have to trust that I do. Cross my heart." He placed his hand over my heart and held it there for a few minutes, wrapped his other arm around my waist pulling me closer to him. He began swaying our bodies to the muffled sounds coming from Club 43. Our bubble intact. We stayed like this for a few songs, enjoying each other's closeness. Max and Smith moved inside the car doing God knew what, so we were in no hurry to bust up their alone time. It was a beautiful night. The stars were out. A slight nip was in the air, but comfortable. Jace and I kept swaying to the music, but then I felt him tense. Oh no hopefully gorilla man was not coming to start trouble again. I looked up to see two police officers patrolling around the club. They were monitoring the crowd outside. They announced, "Half hour until closing people, they aren't admitting anyone else. Time to move on." Jace was stunned still and as I attempted to move he tightened his grip on me. "Babe? Hello? Are ya in there?" I said sarcastically trying to grab his attention, but I grabbed the attention of the police officers instead. "Ma'am, is everything all right?" he said and I nodded not sure if I was telling the truth or not. Jace tensed more as if he were posing for an ice sculpture. He broke out into a cold sweat and my concern grew. "Baby, are you ok?" I said in a shaky tone, willing myself not to freak out. My worry must've brought him out of that dark place, because he shook his

A Minor Happy Ending

head and looked down at me. He spoke slowly while cradling my face in his hands, "I'm sorry Sugar. Was off in my own little world for a minute." Feeling re-assured I grabbed his hand and nodded to the officer in thanks. We were heading to the car when the officer said, "Son? You been drinking?" Oh shit, the cop thought he was drunk, but he hadn't even had a sip all night. He replied "No sir, just tired is all." Skeptically the officer looked him over and realized that he was speaking the truth and waved us along, but not before saying, "Hey. You're that waitress at The Diner, aren't ya?" I nodded and smiled hoping that would speed up our retreat. I needed to find out what that was about. "Well, I'll definitely see you around kiddo. Be careful driving home." I smiled and waved at the nice policeman and said, "Good night."

Chapter 25

 Jace was quiet the entire drive to Max's place, I watched him the whole way. His words said that he was tired, but his body told an entirely different story all on its own. His jaw and neck muscles were tense. His back was rigid and his hands hadn't stopped ringing the steering wheel since we left. His eyes were darting in all directions, checking mirrors continuously like he was going to miss something. This behavior was giving me anxiety. I reached across the seat and began massaging his neck to relieve some stress. He leaned into my touch, but still remained tense. I used my other hand to change the radio station. I found a rock ballad we both loved and a smile pulled at his lips. His calloused hand grasped mine from the back of his neck and he entwined our fingers. When he brought them to his lips and placed a tender kiss to my hand, no words were spoken. No words were needed.

A Minor Happy Ending

We dropped Max and Smith off at her house and I noticed the house was dark. "Oh is Nick out tonight?" I asked out of pure curiosity. Max replied as she opened the door, "Ya, Smith and I have the whole weekend to ourselves. Nick and some friends from work are going to a cabin near the ski resort, looking for girls. Ya know, something about single horny boys and getting laid? Who knows?" "Uh huh, got it." I replied and chanced a glance at the driver and he was just glaring at me.

God, I couldn't win!

We said our goodbyes, the silence returned. It seemed like forever, but I was sure it was only a few minutes before he spoke. "So?" He said with a question in his tone and a glare to match on his face. "So?" I repeated back to him unable to decipher what his problem could've been. "Well, I'm just wondering what the fuck I'm doing wrong here Dyl?" with malice and fear in his tone. Shocked by his blatant asinine question, I wasn't sure what to say, "Other than your mood swings and caveman tendencies not a whole hell of a lot! Why would you ask dearest? Do you feel unappreciated? Do I not show you enough attention, babe? Is it that time of the month? Do you need some Mandol?" I spat with venomous intent. I was a bit tired of these emotional ups and downs. I just wanted to dance with my friend and it turned into a big fiasco as always.

I had the vagina, right?

"Well, obviously I'm not doing enough since we have to go to clubs to dance with guys and keep tabs on your ex boyfriend! For fucks sake Dyl, want me to take you to find him?" he roared.

"Are you fucking serious?" was all I could muster to say at the moment. Continuing he said, "I go out of my way to be with you Dyl, don't you get it!" Out of his way? Really! Fuck this!

After that outburst, there was nothing left to say and silence filled the car again. My blood was boiling, I could hardly contain my anger when the car slowly came to a stop. Before I could totally comprehend what I was doing, I opened the door in haste and walked so fast that my legs felt like they could give out. I yelled toward my Century, "Don't do me any fucking favors, Jace!" All the while I heard him yelling my name and cursing his.

Good! What the fuck did that mean, out of his way?

Before I knew it I was near a familiar place, I tried to sneak in the back door unnoticed, but no such luck. "Dyl, hey girl what are you doing here? It's your night off. You'd think you'd be sick of this place." Becca said with her sweet smile. Her expression changed, when she finally took in

A Minor Happy Ending

my appearance, her smile faltered, and worry lined her face. "Are you all right Dyl?" she said somberly. "Ya I just need to hide for a little while. So, I'm not here, okay?" I practically begged. A sympathetic smile touched her lips, she nodded as she left the break room area. I sat myself on the dusty old lounger in the break room and put up my feet as the dust settled. The couch smelled like grease and old basement. Old reruns of I love Lucy were on the TV, I stared at that ridiculous world and wished it were mine. I closed my eyes and breathed deep, I slowly exhaled and heard a commotion outside of the break room. I heard familiar voices growing louder and then silence. The break room opened, Becca peeked her head in and just nodded. I closed my eyes, disappeared into my thoughts until I drifted off into a Lucy coma and eventually to sleep.

Sometime later I was awakened with warm tickles of air on my neck, spilling the sweetest words known to mankind causing my body to heat. My heart knew who was bringing me out of my fog when I felt soft kisses trailing down my ear, then further down my neck. "I'm so sorry baby, so sorry. Please show me those beautiful blue eyes." I knew I shouldn't give in so easy, but he could always get me to do things I normally wouldn't do. He was worth it. Worth everything. I blinked then found tear filled blue eyes meeting mine. His dirty blonde hair a mess from undoubtedly repeated self-mutilation, I hated when he messed with those short locks. His calloused hands roamed until they landed behind my neck lifting me until our lips touched. Holding me there, staring into my eyes, keeping my lips hostage in limbo. They were barely touching when I could no longer take his reluctance and pressed my eager lips to his. The pressure was light and sensual as his lips and tongue skated over mine. He smelled like a hint of smoke and soap like Jace always did. The contact caused our bodies to react to one another as only we did. He broke the connection, settled himself between my legs on this dingy break room couch resting his head on my chest listening to my body's reaction to him. I knew he did this at times. When he thought I was asleep he rested his head on my chest and listened to my heart. At first I wasn't sure what he was trying, but then he would accompany my heart beat with a rhythm of his own that he would lightly drum on my chest with his fingers. Then I noticed a pattern to this ritual, on nights he couldn't sleep or seemed stressed. When he openly began drumming along my skin lightly with his fingers, I realized he didn't realize he was doing it and just pet his dark blonde locks massaging his scalp. He visibly relaxed and

A Minor Happy Ending

his breathing evened out. He murmured, "I'm so sorry, it's just I love you so much Dyl."

What else was there to say, but "I know, I love you, baby." We just lay there for the next couple of hours on our dingy little piece of heaven. I almost forgot everything that happened. Almost, but I allowed myself a minute to enjoy our minor happy ending.

Chapter 26

A few days later

"Dyl, you have a customer?" I heard Becca's voice echo from the front of the kitchen. I decided to help, Mae, the cook clean since it was slow tonight. Bar rush was vacant. No drunken frat boys or stoners to line my pockets this evening. I washed my hands in the back and made sure that I didn't have any grease on my uniform from the traps out back, then neared the front of the restaurant to try to earn my keep. I rounded the corner to see a burly older man, maybe around forty-two with a beard lining his jaw. He'd be hot, ya know, if he wasn't old. It was the nice policeman from the other night. His large brown eyes were kind and creased near the edges from years of smiling. His relaxed presence was inviting and the smile that tugged at his lips was warm and comforting. He was speaking with someone when I approached his table, his smile brightened and he looked genuinely happy to see me.

A Minor Happy Ending

"Well well well, isn't it my favorite bar fly turned waitress." I smiled at him and said. "In the flesh. What can I get for my favorite man in blue?" He chuckled and asked for coffee and water. I fulfilled his drink order and left some extra creamer and sugar on the table just in case. I asked for his food order and was rewarded with the sweetest look when he said with sarcasm, "Well waitress. That is your name? I guess since you haven't told me anything different." I laughed at his goofy line and said, "Dyllan, sir." Looking a bit concerned he leaned toward me and said, "Dyllansir? A bit unconventional, but I think we can work with it. I've heard worse" What a character! "Dyllan" I corrected and genuinely smiled at the kind man. "Ah, well that sounds much better and let's keep the sirs under wraps. You can call me Joe." I smiled when he continued, "and I'm going to call you Pickles." My eyes must've widened a bit, because his smile widened and a chuckle passed his lips. I was sure I could handle a nice man like him calling me pickles. It was kind of funny. Only one other person ever called me pickles and he ran out of our lives years ago, although I liked the name coming from Joe. "Pickles it is, Joe. Now what can I get ya?" I took his order of pancakes and bacon making sure everything was just right for my friend Joe. He enjoyed his food, I made light conversation with him. I found out that he'd never been married and just moved here from Michigan. Us

Ohioans were born and bred to hate all things Michigan, but I could make an exception for Joe. He told me about his dog Kaycee which was a 10 year old yellow lab and the love of his life. Man this guy needed to get some. I told him a little about school, Jenna, Mom and Jace and realized that he dragged more out of me in an hour than most people did in years. He laughed at my stories of my crazy baby sister and seemed genuinely happy to listen. When his lunch hour was up he said, "It was good talking with you Pickles." headed back into work, patrolling the streets and keeping us safe.

   Not long after he left, Max, Jade and Cam strolled into The Diner with a glazed over look in their eyes. I decided to play hostess and grabbed three menus asking them if it was only those three. All three nodded their heads, I sat them at a table in my section to reprieve the other waitresses from having to serve my influenced friends. I leaned my hip into the table and propped my elbow on Jade's chair and asked my friends, "What'll you have babes?" Like it ever changes, all three wanted their coffee with gallons of cream and sugar. Max ordered pancakes and knowing she won't eat them all Jade ordered nothing and would finish them off. It had been like this for years. Cam was quiet, so I looked in her direction and perked my brows in question. Her eyes were following something, I didn't realize what it was until she said with a giggle, "I'll have what you're having." With a puzzled look on my face, I followed her eyes to find my Jace standing near the entrance to the restaurant. The fire in my belly from her nasty comment as well as my personal walking sex toy that entered the building, I replied with vengeance, "He all ready has more than he can handle and loves every minute of it. You might want to find someone with lower standards. Can I interest you in the French toast instead?" Her eyes blazed and her mouth hung open as well as Jades, when Max retorted, "Dyllan really? Not nice, she was just messing with you." Jace walked up behind me sensing the tension in the room and said with a wicked gleam in his eyes, "Hello future Mrs. Harvey," as he wrapped his arms around my waist and placed a kiss to my neck. The icing on the cake was the look on Cam's face. All the color drained from the all ready pale skin causing her to resemble the walking dead, her eyes widened with curiosity, and her mouth hung so low a small bird could've made a nest. He wasn't going to let her pop our bubble. This caused my heart to soar, but as I felt myself sprout imaginary wings Cam had to clip them right off. "Well since you two love birds are so eager to move forward in your relationship, you can do it in your own place. Jace, I'll give you a week, but then you got to get out."

Jace looked devastated, I could tell that he wanted to beg her to change her mind. Although he wouldn't, because of me. He wouldn't want to disappoint me. I should've given him the same respect. This was my entire fault. If I could've just handled my jealousy, he wouldn't be homeless in a weeks' time. He couldn't afford anything decent and I wasn't ready to be out on my own yet. I had to pay for school and help my mom. I was positive that mom wouldn't let him stay with us; she was old fashioned that way. She didn't press her beliefs on me, but I could guarantee that she wouldn't allow it in her home. I opened my mouth to eat some serious crow when Cam stood and walked out. Slowly Max and Jade followed wordlessly, shaking their heads at me and patting my shoulder. My shoulders slumped, I dropped my eyes to the ground in shame. How could I have done this to Jace? All he did was take care of me and take my side no matter what, all I did was make his world a bitter place. I felt two inches tall, but then strong hands engulfed my face lifting it so I could see into his deep blue eyes and he whispered, "Dyl it's okay we're in this together. Hey, we've got a week. A lot can happen in a week and I'm okay as long as I have you." I panicked and explained, "I don't think my mom will let

A Minor Happy Ending

you stay with me. She loves you, don't get me wrong, but she is weirdly old fashioned about that stuff. When she doesn't have to see it, it's one thing but ..." I trailed off unable to speak anymore afraid of how his face would look. I didn't want to cause him anymore trouble. Taking my hand Jace led me through the now vacant restaurant, into the back room we christened a few months back. As soon as the doors closed his mouth his on mine, I felt the door against my back. I felt the need to climb him until both my legs were wrapped around his waist and a groan escaped my throat. He answered my groan with a deeper more feral version of his own. Our hands were everywhere. I wasn't sure where he began and I ended. The fire in my belly grew south and was no longer burning, but blazing, I couldn't control myself. As my nimble fingers undid his jeans I felt him tear my underwear to shreds. His need for me was fierce and I could feel it down to my toes. I pulled him free and with one swift movement he was buried deep inside me. There were no sweet kisses or caresses, this was pure punishing need. He was taking out all his aggression and worry out on me and Oh my God was I loving every minute of it. His speed and strength never faltered as he held me up against that door, taking everything he needed from me. I gave and I gave until both of us crashed onto the most gratifying experience a human being could have. We fell apart together in a crumpled pile onto the floor. Never once wondering if anyone could've seen or heard our exchange and not really caring at the moment. He protected me in his arms claiming his love for me all over again, I listened to it with the enthusiasm of a child hearing her favorite bed time story. "One day it will be easy. We will have our own home with our own family and no one can pop our bubble, Sugar. Don't you see that, I had to prove to you that it was still here. It'll always be here Dyl. It was our bubble. The only ones who can pop it is us" he said passionately. I lifted my eyes and pressed my lips to his unable to respond to his perfect words. I doubted that I could ever do him justice for the love he had shown me these last six months and it just caused me to love him more.

We dressed quickly and he took a seat at the table that my friends had vacated and I was much more pleased with the company that I had now. He was beautiful and more relaxed than I had seen him in a while. He relaxed in the booth and watched me complete my dining room duties. I made a show of bending over, leaning over the tables showing a small amount of cleavage. I guess it was a bit pointless since he all ready got the milk without buying the cow, but it was still fun to tease. Once my work was finished, I helped lock up with Jace in tow and said, "C'mon we are not going to Cam's tonight. I know of the perfect place, but we need to stop by my place first."

A Minor Happy Ending

Chapter 27

The Century got us home safely, but Mom's car wasn't in the driveway and I began to worry. Jace noticed the worried look on my face and quickly ushered me inside. No words were spoken while I frantically searched the house for any signs of them, when I saw a half ripped sheet of paper lying on my bed.

Dyl

Gran called and was feeling ill. Jenna and I went to spend the weekend with her. She said it's just the flu ,but I want to make sure she's fine. If you need anything, call or text me. I hope to actually SEE my beautiful daughter when I get back. Dinner Sunday night at 8 and yes bring Jace.

Love you more than ice cream

Mom

Man, I missed her, but Jace playing house with me all weekend long would be amazing, without Cam it'd be even better! I handed him the letter, he read it with a smile that displayed across his lips. As he attempted to control his elation, he said, "Sorry to hear about your Gran", as his arms snaked around my body. "Ya, me too." I feigned concern. Not that I didn't have concern for Gran. She was amazing, but I also know Gran was a tremendous faker when she wanted attention. Hopefully, she wasn't crying wolf. "We have the house to ourselves for two days." "Ok baby, what do we do first?" A large smile appeared on his face and his hands began roaming, I pulled away even though every instinct that I had told me to strip him bare and to have my way with him. I had this overwhelming urge to take a nice warm shower, "Well I'm going to shower and then maybe we should grab a quick bite to eat before bed." I said not totally comfortable with screwing all over my mom's house.

After a long shower, I reluctantly left the warm confines of my bathroom and stepped out onto the small green woven rug. I wrapped my towel around my head and made my own version of a turban to help dry my hair, then grabbed another towel to wrap around my body. The smell of my strawberry shampoo filtered through the room and the steam was rising. I opened the door in the hallway and the steam began to billow out of the bathroom and into the hall. The smell of mint carried into the hall, I smiled finding Jace sniffing the air and smiling back in my direction. "I love that smell sugar. I could inhale your smell all day. If you were in that shower any longer I was going to have to come in there and smell you first hand." he drawled. If I wasn't already wet from my shower, this would've caused the same result.

He sauntered up to me and wrapped his arms around my waist, and continued with his sweet words, "I don't know what I would do without your sweet smell and kind heart Dyl." pointing at my chest, he continued, "This is my home, you are my home. Where ever we are, baby that's where home is." I melted into his embrace and pressed my lips into his firm chest. "I love you, babe, my heart has been and always will be yours." I whispered in his chest. We stood there holding each other for a few minutes and from what had started as a heated exchange turned a somber note. I couldn't help but ask again. "Baby, please tell me what's going on. I know something isn't right. You've been acting strange. You don't want to go anywhere. You are always looking over your shoulder when we go places. Please, babe, tell me. Are your parents searching for you? Maybe it's time to face them. Tell them that you are an adult now and that you will decide where you want to live. I don't want you to regret not having a relationship with them. Then maybe they will wait to leave until you start school." A mixture of emotions presented across his face as he stared in my eyes, but the most apparent was fear. "I,... I can't Dyl. I, ... I'll lose you. I can't lose you, baby." He somberly whispered with tears filling his eyes, when the first one spilled, I couldn't help but reassure him that that was the last thing that could ever happen, he was my reason for breathing most days and my world would've been turned upside down without him in it. I reminded him that he was my home and I never wanted to be without him. I reminded him that one day we would grow old together and count each other's wrinkles and sugar rush our grand babies. I reminded him that was our future no matter what happened next. As his tears subsided, he looked into my eyes with so much fear and exhaustion. He reached into his back pocket and pulled out a newspaper clipping, slowly opening the folded paper and handed it to me wordlessly. His hands shook as he finally laid the paper in my hand and set his sights on the floor.

What could be so bad? His parents placed an ad looking for him?

A Minor Happy Ending

Then I looked down to find the headline, MOST WANTED, Jace Harvey with a picture of him below with a short article explaining that he failed to appear to his probation appointment and now had a warrant out for his arrest. It explained that he was on probation for Domestic assault to his father and only had eight months left on his probation when he failed to appear, which was five months ago.

POP!

Five months? No that couldn't be. We just got together, when this happened. He wouldn't lie to me for this long.

As I finished reading the article I looked up into his eyes and saw that he did. He lied. He couldn't even keep eye contact with me at this point as tears began to filter through and spill over my lids. I lost all will to stand, crumbled to the ground in my towel and sobbed. He lowered himself to me and hugged me so close that I felt smothered. I let him stay with me like this for I don't know how long because I knew I wouldn't have this much longer. He would be leaving me. Even though not by choice, but he would. The sadness was overwhelming and all I could do was whisper, "What do we do now?" He rocked me and just hummed. Knowing that we wouldn't have much more time together, he just kept humming and rocking me into the early hours of the morning. We drifted off to sleep in the hallway, me in a towel and him completely dressed.

I awoke a bit cold from where we were and jostled Jace to wake up, so we could go to bed. I was officially in shock right now.

What were those stages on grief again? Denial, anger, bargaining, depression and acceptance.

Well, I was pretty sure I jumped straight to depression. I was broken. My heart was in shreds and the only thing that could help it was also the man that caused it. How could he have lied to me? For five months? How? How could he have asked me for a future when he wasn't even sure if he had one? What was so important that he had to blow off his probation appointment? My heart plummeted and I felt the burn of anger rising as I lead him into my room. My breathing became more rapid, my fists clenched as he sat himself on my bed. I felt my face heat and my whole body tensed and when his eyes met mine, he saw it too. His eyes widened waiting for my rath, when I began pounding on his chest and yelling at him as loud as I could, "How could you? How could you lie to me, Jace? Five months? Five fucking months, you've hidden something from me? What future do you think we have now? Huh? Monthly conjugal visits? I get to visit my husband in the big house and explain to our children that their daddy is just a big fat liar. What the fuck Jace? Is that why you asked me to marry you? So, you knew I'd be there after you got caught. FUCK Jace! What were you thinking? You are going to fix this! Either you fix this or I have to go!" During my entire rant, he kept his eyes to the ground and shook his head. When he looked up at me and whispered, "I'm so sorry Sugar. I was afraid to tell you. I was afraid I'd lose you." My anger had risen and I bit back, "Don't fucking call me that! Not today. No sweet words can change what you've done. FUCK Jace, you could've gotten me in so much trouble. Do you not even care about my part in this? What was so fucking important that you missed your appointment?" His head dropped again and answered in a small voice, "You remember that day, Smith and I surprised you at the beach? I told you that I blew something off..." He trailed off and looked at me under heavy lids when I exploded, "ARE YOU FUCKING KIDDING ME? You blew off your probation so you could surprise me at the beach! Are you fucking serious?" he nodded and responded, "All I kept thinking about was you at the beach and all of those other guys there that aren't on probation and that are better than me. I couldn't let anyone else get to you Dyllan. I can't be without you. I was right, though. When I got there, you already had a guy there trying to take you away." "Take me away? I had no intention of doing anything with that guy, he was nothing because he wasn't you. All this time, I thought this was about your parents. I thought they were searching for you.

I thought you'd tell me about it when you were ready. But you've made it perfectly clear that I meant nothing because you couldn't even respect me enough to tell me the truth. You let your jealousy and insecurity lead your mind instead of your heart. That's not the man I love." He had risen and made his way toward the door as he proclaimed "it's because you're my everything." I watched as his shoulders slumped and his eyes never left the floor, when he walked slowly to the door and said, "I love you Sugar," and left.

What was he doing? Was he leaving? Where did he think he was going?

I waited a few more minutes, when he didn't return I opened the front door to see him walking away from me when panic took over and I couldn't breathe! My chest tightened and my heart was pounding. Before I realized what I was doing, I was running as fast as my feet would carry me down the street without shoes and only a towel to cover me as I was yelling his name. He turned around and relief washed over him as he slumped his shoulders in defeat and gathered me into his arms, carrying me back home kissing my lips, my chin and my neck with such desperation that both of our bodies were vibrating.

A Minor Happy Ending

I couldn't let him go. I just couldn't. It felt like the air was being sucked from my lungs. I was still angry, so very angry, but now I could breathe.

I whispered, "We'll fix this baby, we'll fix it together, but no more lies. Promise me." It was more of a command than a question and as fast as he could respond, "Promise." We fell asleep in a tangle of arms, legs and lips. He was home. I was his. We needed to figure out how to fix our home. I didn't know what we were going to do, but we'd figure it out together.

Shaan Ranae

Chapter 28

Light filtered in through the curtains and settled on my face bathing me in its warmth, giving me a false sense of comfort. Inhaling the scent of Jace and my room was a heavenly intoxicating mixture that caused an insatiable need deep down. I opened my eyes to his beautiful face featuring a shadow around his jaw accentuating the already beautiful man. His deep breathes and listless motions were captivating and I tentatively reached up to touch his face. As my fingers skated along his jaw and landed on his pink lips caressing them as if they'd disappear at a moment's notice, I appreciated the feel of his stubble on my fingers. I wasn't a deeply religious person but I had my own relationship with God. I believed he gave Jace to me for a reason. This man was mine and every heart beat that my corrupted muscle made beat only for him, so I prayed. "Please God, don't take him from me. I'll help Mom and Jenna more. I'll volunteer more. I'll be the best nurse you'll ever see, I promise. Please help us figure this out. I can't lose him. Thank you for giving him to me. Help us make the right decisions. Please, please let me keep him. I can't imagine my life without him."

When I uttered the last of my whispered words, Jace stirred and I found myself captured in his limbs and loving the feel of my man wrapped around me. Feeling the wetness on my cheeks caused realization that tears must've fallen, since I was not sure how long I had left with him. I wiped my cheeks dry with the sheets and inhaled his scent. I found my place tucked into his nook. It felt like it was made to fit only me. It was my nook. I got comfortable and he began to hum. He was awake now and we weren't moving, enjoying each other's embrace for the time being. He began running his fingers through my strawberry blonde locks as he hummed my song and placed feather light kisses to my head. I reveled in the feeling of his warmth, comforting me and reassuring me that we would be okay. The emotions running through me became too powerful and I could no longer hold onto what I was feeling when I began to openly sob. His arms wrapped tighter as he begged me by whispering over and over again, "Baby I'm so sorry. Please. I'll fix this. Please don't be sad because of me. You're my heart. You're my reason for breathing. I love you so much Dyl. Please." I continued to sob for what seemed like hours and allowed him to continue to comfort and love me with his sweet caresses and whispers until there were no tears left. My mind wandered to the past six months as some of the happiest in my life and I grieved for what came next not ready for the fight and the uncertainty to come. Not ready to grow up yet and face a reality that I didn't completely understand. I wanted to believe that we could've beaten anything and that he would've found a way to stay with me.

Stay? Where are we going to stay? Ugh! I was going to have to move out. I didn't know what else he'd do. If I wasn't so hell bent on being a colossal bitch to Cam, he'd still have a place to stay. Everything would've been fine if I would've just kept my big mouth shut. I broke my silence and whispered, "I'm so sorry baby." He froze and flipped me to face him. Vehemence in his voice as he placed his hands on both sides of my jaw holding me in place he said, "You don't apologize. I'm the asshole here. I screwed up. I'll fix this, because I'm not losing you." A stray tear fell down his cheek and I reached up to wipe it free, while mine ran freely down my face and I couldn't control my sobbing to the point of hiccups and guttural noises. He rubbed his hands along my spine giving comfort and taking comfort from me in return.

When I had no more tears, we climbed out of bed and made our way into the kitchen where I proceeded to make

A Minor Happy Ending

him breakfast. Nothing special, just strawberry and banana yogurt smoothies and wheat toast. He quickly gulped it up with a smile as if it was a gourmet treat, which brought a smile to my face. These sweet moments shared should be appreciated since I wasn't sure how many we would have left. He looked at me knowingly as if he could read my mind and said, "Dyl baby, we will figure this out. I'm not giving up on us. Now, please stop looking at me like it's the last time you'll ever see me. We've been okay for this long. We can make it a little longer until we can find a way out of this." I felt reluctance and fear take over when I asked, "Well how much longer do you plan to keep me at risk here, Jace? I can get into so much trouble. Does it even bother you? What about my nursing degree? Do you think I'll be hirable after a felony under my belt? I love you baby, I do but what is the plan? I can't go on forever this way." His shoulders slumped, his head dropped and his eyes scanned the floor in shame. I wasn't meaning to scold him or shame him, but everything I had been working toward had been fucked with and I was scared and frankly a bit pissed. I continued, "Do you maybe think it's time to call your parents?" he looked up instantly afraid, like the police were outside my door. "Or a fucking lawyer? God Jace. Anyone?" His eyes lit up and I could almost see the wheels turning when he blurted out, "Where's your phone book?" I pointed to the coffee table and murmured, "Under the lid" and watched as he flipped through so many pages, I wasn't so sure that he knew who he was looking for, then he finally stopped searching and smacked the page. "Can I use your phone?" he said enthusiastically. I nodded and waited patiently as he dialed and spoke adamantly with someone he seemed somewhat familiar with since he was cracking mild jokes and thanking him repeatedly. I sat there staring at him until he hung up and hurriedly walked over to where I was sitting and dropped to his knees wrapping his arms around me and resting his head on my lap. The way he looked as he came my way was relieved. He looked freaking relieved and now he was silent. His posture was more relaxed and his breathing had deepened and yet I was still in the dark. Oh fuck this! "Jace?" he nuzzled my lap and made a nonchalant noise in his throat. "Jace, who was that?" I said a little more sternly as I could feel my irritation rise and my muscles tensed. He breezily said, "Oh it was Fred." "Okay, well who the fuck is Fred?" I quickly barked back no longer enjoying his breezy attitude. He chuckled in my lap and as I was about to grab a handful of his dark blonde hair, he looked up with those dark blue eyes and floored me. The worry that had been there for the last six months had dissipated and his cocky grin was in place. How I had missed his worry free face. He was so beautiful, I almost forgot that he was annoying the crap out of me. Almost.

A Minor Happy Ending

"Jace Harvey, If I don't have an explanation in about two seconds, you are not going to like me very much." He chuckled again and said, "He's the dad of a friend of mine from school. He's aware of my situation and is willing to help me straighten this out." I felt a smile spread across my face and faux security, when I asked, "Well what did he say? Is he hopeful that you'll be okay?" He nodded and said, "He says that I should turn myself in right away and I'll be better off. I won't do that though. I asked him to speak with my probation officer first and see if she will plea bargain with him, then I will turn myself in. If we can get her to be lenient hopefully the judge will be too." I looked at him in disbelief. "But if he says you should go now, then maybe…." I trailed off not wanting him to get the wrong idea. He looked at me in disbelief and said, "It's all ready been six months Dyl, not expecting too much help from her but I have to try before I'm ripped away from you. Ya know I could barely breathe for that short walk down the road last night. If I go in now it could be months away from you. I'm not sure I can go months without breathing you in, touching your hair, or tasting your skin. Just please baby, I have to call him back tomorrow to see what she said, so for now let's see. This as a step in the right direction, okay?" I was nodding before I could actually absorb the reality of the situation and he leaned up into my embrace and held me while humming my song.

This felt so good and I knew what he meant I couldn't breathe either, I felt like I was suffocating. It was a miserable feeling and I never wanted to feel that again. So what was one more day, we could take this step and maybe another tomorrow.

A Minor Happy Ending

Chapter 29

We spent the day watching old movies and eating microwave popcorn for lunch and dinner. He played his guitar and sang for me a few times, making me sing along. I wasn't horrible, but I definitely didn't have Jace's soulful tone and sound. We took a few naps and cuddled on the couch. This gave me a glimpse into what a lazy Saturday would've felt like when we got older and had our own home. Then when we were ready our little spawn would crawl up onto our laps as Jace sang them to sleep and I petted their strawberry blonde hair as I gazed into their little dark blue eyes. That was something I wouldn't mind looking forward to when we got all of this mess settled, but that was another day.

It was getting dusky outside and the sun began to set. Jace was surrounding me and the lull of the TV was slowly putting me to sleep. I felt his hands wander down my frame causing goose bumps to form across my skin. His calloused warm hands wandering down my hips, caressing my ass and finding my warmth from behind, gently massaging my heat drenching my undies, caused him to groan in response. His groan awakened a feral need in me, one that I couldn't control. I was suddenly straddling his waist and grinding my warmth on his hard cock. The more I grind the harder he got and the wetter I became. Our tongues and lips collided with rough hurried kisses, like we were trying to fit a lifetime of love making into a few hours. My movements became jerky and my body felt like convulsing when my orgasm flooded through my entire body. Jace was holding me as if he was protecting me from the evils of the world. When reality hits that we hadn't even undressed yet and I'd left his jeans with an extremely large wet spot. He looked down and his cocky crooked smile was in place, when he said, "WOW, sugar I've really been neglecting you if you came that hard without me inside that sweet pussy of yours." I melted a little more at the sex dripping from those lips of his, I loved when he used that filthy mouth on me. "Sugar, I need you out of these clothes. I need to taste every single inch of you before I sink into you and stay for as long as you'll let me. I don't think my cock has ever been so hard and I don't want to come until you come in my mouth and on my cock." I felt the flood between my legs before he felt it and a guttural groan came from his throat and my underwear was torn from my body, my shirt pulled over my head so quickly before I even registered his mouth on my breast. Alternating between nipping and lapping at my nipple made me whimper with need for him, while taking his time cherishing my body like it was his temple, like I was his reason for living. There was nothing sexier than when Jace worshiped me. As he switched to my other breast his hand began to travel south and was met with a moist heat. His fingers delved into my wetness causing a shiver throughout my core. His fingers thrusted while his mouth caressed my breasts with determination. His mouth began descending kisses down my stomach, over my hips while he massaged my sex with his hands. When his mouth met my pussy his tongue took a tentative swipe making my hips jerk off the couch. Then his hands grabbed my hips forcing them down and holding me still so I absorbed all the pleasure. I felt like my hips were stuck in a vice when his whole mouth descended on my pussy as he alternated licking and sucking my clit. He owned my body. He was playing me like I was his own personal instrument. His guitar had nothing on me! I gasped when I felt his teeth nibbling on my clit and his fingers found my core and began to fuck me relentlessly. My orgasm shot through my body as I screamed out his name and tightened my thighs around his head. My hips still immobile kept relief from the excruciating pleasure that I was unable to stop as wave after wave of sensation would not subside. He licked up all evidence of my orgasm and he kissed his way up my body. In one perfect thrust he was deep inside me. I could feel his balls smacking against my ass as he began to powerfully but slowly gaining his pleasure from me. "Sugar, you are sweeter every time I taste you and the way you fit my cock is perfect. Your sweet pussy is mine. Tell me who owns this, Dyl." He rasped in my ear as his powerful controlled movements brought me closer to another release. I whispered, "You." He chuckled and shook his head with his crooked grin in place, "Dyl, say it right baby. Say my name. Let me know this is only mine that for all eternity I own you. Your pussy, your mind and your heart. I want it all, Dyl. All of it. Now tell me Sugar, who owns this sweet body?"

 "You do Jace, it's all yours. It's only ever been yours." I admitted effortlessly knowing that it was true. That man owned not only my body but he owned my soul. After I proclaimed my undying need for him Jace's control faltered and his movement became less controlled and more wild as if he was digging deeper and deeper into not only my body but into my soul. When I felt his release inside me, my core began to contract as we both finished together. He collapsed on top of me and whispered, "I love you Sugar, we'll have our happy ending. We'll have it. I'll fix everything. I want a life with you, you're my everything." I petted his head as it rested on my chest as it raised and fell rapidly from our love making. "I know baby" was all I could say as my throat thickened and I fought the tears that weren't needed at this time. The hope in his face was what was needed now. We might not have had our happy ending yet, but that day we had a minor one.

Chapter 30

The rest of the weekend was amazing and then mom and Jenna returned from Grandma's. As I thought, Grandma wanted some extra attention, but I was glad they had a good visit with her. The dinner with Mom and Jenna went well with them telling stories from their exciting weekend away with Grandma. We laughed and told Jace a few silly memories that lit up his face. He looked like that he actually felt comfortable with us. No over politeness or flirtiness, just sweet Jace experiencing us Prescott girls. Knowing he had to find somewhere to stay tonight, I even tried asking my mom if he could stay on the couch for a couple of days and she agreed. He better get this straightened out soon or I'd be disowned. Mom didn't like the fact that he had nowhere to stay, but made it clear that it was on the couch and only for a couple of days. I was relieved when Smith said he could stay at his house for a little while, which eased my mind some. I could go home at night and not worry about him. I didn't want Mom to find out what was going on. She would've been so disappointed, but she wouldn't have understood the situation. She'd tell me to have him turn himself in so I wouldn't get into trouble. I didn't want her to dislike him.

A few weeks go by and Jace was spending a lot of time at The Diner while I was working. My boss, John was starting to ask me why he was here all night and holding up one of his tables. I gave him a good enough explanation to drop the subject for now, but made a mental note to say something to Jace. When I looked over at the table I saw Jace speaking with someone and was alarmed the moment I realized who he was speaking with. I walked cautiously to the table with an eerie smile plastered on my face, when he spoke, "Hey pickles. How 'bout a cup of Joe?" he said using his name as a play on words. "Ya want me to squeeze the cow too?" I asked in our in our weird little way if he wanted milk. "You know better than that" he said with condescension. As he falsely chastised me for forgetting his coffee order, I gave Jace a weary look. He patted my hand with a reassuring smile in place, whispering loudly across the table to Joe, "Ya know Joe, she is getting older and they say the memory is the first thing to go," Joe chuckled and shook his head, telling him that he'd be in so much trouble later. I couldn't help but laugh at them together, but I knew if Joe knew the situation, he would take Jace away. I didn't want Joe to be disappointed in me or put me in jail. Good bye nursing career. Good bye future. I plastered my so called fake smile and took Joe his black coffee. Jace stood and offered his hand to Joe as I approached when Joe said, "Thanks Pickles, now you keep that fella of yours in line now. Oh, and Jace it was nice talking with you. Take good care of her." Jace shook his hand and Joe took his coffee and began reading his paper. Jace retreated to his own table. He started drawing on a napkin and drinking his own cup of coffee. As he was doodling on the napkin, I walked around the corner and let out an exhausted breathe. I made sure I was out of view when I watched the beautifully infuriating man. What was he thinking talking with Joe? What if Joe got curious about Jace? Oh crap, what if he already knew and that was why he befriended me? How could he have been be so careless when we were so close to fixing this? Well at least hopefully fixing this. I hadn't heard an update in a few days and he kept reassuring me that we'd fix this but how was I helping him fix something when I didn't know what in the hell was going on? I needed a break. I was beyond stressed. I was constantly worried if he had a place to sleep for the night or if he had money to eat on. My school work had suffered. I'd barely seen my house except to sleep, but I kept telling myself that it'd all be worth it once he was free. I might as well go to jail because I felt like I was in my own self inflicted incarceration at the moment. I was constantly caring for someone else. Maybe I wasn't ready yet. Jace glanced up searching for me when he saw me staring, he smiled and then that smile faltered. He knew what I was thinking. He raised from the booth ready to confront me, when I scrambled around the corner and headed to the break room. It wasn't the best hiding spot and he'd been back here before. The bitches I worked with loved Jace and would let him back there just to spite me.

A few minutes later, Becca came back and had a look of concern on her pretty face. "NO!" I blurted out knowing Jace sent her after me, so he could go all alpha male on me. "I'm on my break." She rolled her eyes and shrugged at me when she said, "well your fiancé is demanding your presence in the extra dining room." Fiance? Huh? He was throwing that word around like it entitled him my complete attention. Oh I'd go see him all right.

Entering that dining room with a little trepidation and a lot of anger, I crossed my arms and barked out with utter distaste, "You beckoned me master?" He froze glaring at me, wringing his hands together like I just stopped him from the most important prayer he ever prayed. "Well?" I barked out without a word from him. His eyes almost turned black, his neck and ears were flushed red and his chest was heaving. I tried to keep my anger and my desire at bay, but I wasn't an idiot when it came to Jace's reaction to me. I knew he wanted me as much as I wanted him. This time instead of following my lust I was going to listen to my head and let him have it. "You think it's funny to insult that nice old man. You don't think that maybe he could get curious about you? Or as a kindness to me he may want to check you out? Or here's a long shot, maybe I care about what he thinks and don't want to see him disappointed in me. Does it even matter to you that I'm making sacrifices here too. I need a break Jace. I just, I need a break." He peered up at me with unshed tears in his eyes and nodded. He delved his hands in his pockets and began to walk away. He only made it to the back door before my mind started wondering and panic took over. I didn't even realize that I was crying. He shrugged and silently walked toward the door and whispered, "I'm sorry, baby. I love you." I caught up with him and ask, "Where are you going?" Uncertain and afraid, he tilted his head up and looked at me under his lids. "To give you time. Dyl, I don't know where else to go. You are my only home, but I love you and will give you anything I can. If it's a break you need. I'll give it to you." His voice broke on the last word as if it was the hardest thing he'd ever had to say. Then he finished, "I wasn't thinking about how you would be affected by me talking with him. I was hoping he could help us. He already loves you, so I thought if he liked me

A Minor Happy Ending

too then we'd have an ally on our side. I'm trying everything that I can to stay with you." he said with such defeat and hope at the same time. Sometimes I forgot how young we were, when Jace allowed his naivety to show it usually stirred the panic inside of me. I'd always had responsibilities and had to be dependable to others. He'd never had been those things. He had no clue. So, was I going to chastise him for trying to fix this? No I wasn't. "Baby, wait a minute. I know you only have the best intentions but that was too close for comfort. I like Joe. He was so nice, but it was his job to take you in if he knew about you. I don't want him to think badly of me or of you, for that matter. Also, I need to know you are moving toward a better solution to our problem other than befriending my police officer buddy at work. What's going on Jace?" He looked down searching for the right words and then just blurted out, "She said no okay. My probation officer, she said she won't bargain with me and that I will be doing some time. It will be less the sooner I turn myself in. Okay! I'm desperate now, Dyl. I'm so afraid when I turn myself in that you'll realize what a loser I am and leave me. It kills me to think of you not loving me anymore. My parents didn't, why should you?" he ranted with sullen words and a defeated slump. I cautiously approached him and raised my hands to grasp his beautiful face as he reluctantly looked into my eyes.

"Nothing will ever change the fact that I love you Jace Harvey. I can't wait until the day when you place that band on my finger and give me your last name showing the whole world that we belong to each other. Then the days after when we grow older and watch our own babies make the same mistakes we did. Well, hopefully not the exact same ones." I added with a hint of sarcasm. He chuckled and gave me his signature crooked smile. "Jace baby, a few months away from you isn't going to change that." Hurriedly, he grabbed my face and tenderly traced my lips with his, nipping and lapping his tongue along my seam. I opened my mouth a little more and he began to deepen our kiss. Then as quickly as it started, it ended with him smiling and my knees weakened. "Baby, I have to get back to work, but we need to talk this over when I get done." I said with a stern voice and he nodded knowing not all was fixed but was on the right track.

At the end of my shift, I asked him whose couch he'd surf tonight and he shrugged. When I checked my tips and their wasn't enough for a hotel, I didn't have much of a cash flow lately since I was paying for two and helping mom.

We decided we would take the Century somewhere for the night and campout. I stopped at home and grabbed a few blankets. Mom and Jenna were sleeping so I didn't have to explain my quick departure. We drove out to the old make out spot and climbed into the back of the Century and cuddled as we let the day fade away into dreamland.

Knock, knock, knock

Knock, knock, knock

What is that? It wasn't even day light yet?

Knock, knock, knock

Suddenly I realized we were still in my car, when I looked up to see a flashlight and a familiar face knocking on my window. I smiled, but then frowned realizing if Joe was knocking on my car window, it meant that someone reported us for being up here. I nudged Jace as he raised to see Joe tapping on my window and realization hit him too. Thank god we were dressed. I rolled down my window with a meek smile in place and said, "Oh hey Joe, we must've fallen asleep while watching the stars last night." He gave me a knowing smile and said, "Ah, that's what they are calling it these days." I blushed and hid my face with my hands as Jace spoke up, "Joe you remember your first love right. Wanting to spend every waking moment together and wanting to hold your girl in your arms all night." My heart fluttered at his statement as I watched Joe. He rolled his eyes and shook his head. "He's got it bad, Pickles, take it easy on him okay? Now, go home. I ran your plates. I'm going to drive by in an hour to make sure that your car is there. Respect her young man, a lady should never sleep in a car." He said protectively. "Thanks, dad," I said with a mischievous smile and then thanked him properly for the heads up. He smiled and nodded as he tapped his hands on the top of my car twice.

We climbed into the front seat and I started the car to let it warm up when Jace grabbed my hand and squeezed knowing that this had to end soon. We reached my house and I snuck him into my room and locked the door until mom and Jenna left for the day. The fear of her catching him here scared me because I didn't want her to think ill of him now. I couldn't stomach it. Who knew what she'd think after he turned himself in. Jace slept soundly as I showered and made coffee. I enjoyed my third cup when he came into the living room. He sat beside me, wrapping his arms around my waist and dragging me into his lap. "G'mornin Sugar." He said in his sexy gruff morning voice. "Morning" I replied with a little more pep. "Well someone is chipper this morning." I snuggled my nose into his neck capturing his scent to memory like I was never going to smell it again. And a dark feeling replaced my peppy mood immediately when I remembered our predicament last night. "Baby, what are we going to do now?" I asked apprehensively. I didn't want to fight anymore. I didn't want to be afraid anymore. We needed a plan. He exhaled a long breath and then began rubbing firm circles on my

A Minor Happy Ending

back. "Well I see it this way, our one year anniversary is in eight days. We spend a romantic anniversary together and then as your anniversary gift from me I will face the demons head on and turn myself in the day after. We will start our tough fight then, but give me these last eight days. Eight days to hold you. Eight days to kiss you. Eight days of endless orgasms. Eight days to profess my undying love for you. Shit Dyl, if I knew I wouldn't get caught, I'd take you to Vegas today and marry you, but I know that's not right. You deserve your day." I smiled knowing that he had finally heard me. Finally proved to me that he was the man that I knew he was. His words had me melting and then his hands were stripping me of my clothes as he made love to me all afternoon.

Chapter 31

"Bitch, where you been hiding?" I heard the familiar voice of my friend Jade as she walked into my house unannounced as usual. Smiling I greeted her with a hug. "What are you doing here baby girl? I've missed you though." Sympathetically she stated, "Ya I know. That's kind of why I'm here. I was going to wait until Max got here but Dyl, what's going on? I know what his issues are, but why are you getting mixed up in his shit. I know you love the guy, but if he loved you he wouldn't put you through this." I nodded knowing she was right and tried to ease her mind with my words, "Well, we decided last night that the day after our one year anniversary, he will turn himself in. In eight days, I'm going to be a mess." Her eyes widened at this knowledge and sympathy took it's place, "Well Dyl, you'll still have me and Max until lover boy gets out of the slammer. Well, ya never know he may be joining my team when he's there." I must've had a tortured look

A Minor Happy Ending

on my face because Jade quickly retracted her statement in an attempt to comfort me. "Ah shit Dyl, I was just joking. I didn't mean it. I thought I'd make you laugh, you look so worn out." Then a soft knock on the door brought me out of my stupor as I arose from the couch a little big breasted pixie walked in and gave me the biggest bear hug. She always knew when I needed her. It like this sixth sense she had. "Jade, I told you to wait for me didn't I? She looks like you've shot her puppy." She scolded as I squeezed her and that was when the man of the hour stepped out from his shower with just a towel on, leaving all of us speechless. "Hey guys, good to see ya. I'll, uh I'll just go get dressed." smiling at our obvious ogling of his sexy as sin body and stuttering his words. All three of us rubbernecking to watch that sexy man walk down that hall, when Jade said, "Yeah, I'd go straight for that guy, I get it now". We all three erupted into laughter as my two best friends cuddled and consoled me. When Jace came out completely dressed and smelling incredibly yummy, Jade announced, "Are ya ready, man?" "Yep let's go." He said with a knowing smirk. Confused I perked up and asked, "Um what's going on?" "Oh, Jade said she'd help me do something nice for you for our anniversary." He explained as he and Jade were walking through the door and waving goodbye to me and Max.

"Well it's just us chica!" Max exclaimed. "You pop the popcorn, I'll melt the butter. There's an Elvis movie marathon on today!" I jumped, excited to have some girl time. I felt like I'd been ignoring them with all the craziness going on around here lately. Partially because I didn't want to hear them tell me the truth and partially because I didn't want to risk them getting into trouble. Just because I chose this path didn't mean I couldn't protect them from it.

We spent the afternoon watching Elvis movies and catching up. She informed me that she and Smith were in love. I was so happy for her. She also told me that he was amazing in bed. It was always the quiet ones. She told me tales of wild nights and mind blowing orgasms and honestly I was shocked. Props to Smith, never would've guessed it. I was just happy that he made her so happy. She deserved it.

A few hours later, Jace came back with Jade and told me to pack my bags. When I asked what to pack, he said, "I'm perfectly fine with you walking around naked all week." So, I decided to pack a little of everything. Jace gave Jade a hug thanking her for her help and then Max for bringing my spirits up. He then informed them that he was relying on them to keep me company until he got back so I wasn't

A Minor Happy Ending

lonely. They nodded and smiled as they left us to get ready for our trip.

We hopped in the car, our bags in the back. I left mom a note and told her that I'd return in a week but to call me if she needed anything. I was so glad she trusted me to make the right choices but lately I felt like I kept letting her down. She didn't know it and hopefully never will. After he turned himself in, I'd sit down with her and explain it all. She'd understand. She was young and in love once. Jace drove us up all the curvy roads leading to a secluded area with four or five cabins nestled in this little nook. It was so cozy and private. I looked at him astonished and asked, "How in the world could you afford this Babe?" He smiled and said, "I always have a backup plan sugar." I shook my head at his cocky comment and felt that tingling sensation in my belly anticipating our mini vacation. We reached the cabin and he pulled the key from his jeans. He turned the key and opened the door, then effortlessly lifted me over the threshold. My lips met his in a fury of lips, teeth and tongues. Wanting him on me, around me and in me all at once, I started peeling his clothes from his body. His movements matching mine in perfect harmony. My shirt then his, my pants then his, my underwear then his, then I almost orgasmed as my hand rubbed against his hardness. I could hardly control myself when I heard myself beg. "Hard baby, throw me down and fuck me hard. Make me forget what is coming next. Don't let me think anymore, just make me feel you. All of you." I needed him more than my next breath. Next thing I knew, I am slammed on the bed, then rolled onto my stomach. One hard slap to my ass perked my head up, when he lifted my hips and slammed inside of me from behind. No warning. No prep. Just his hardness ramming into me, punishing me over and over with a mixture of pain and pleasure that I'd never experienced in my life and as if he could feel my orgasm about to erupt I felt a moist finger near my little forbidden whole and he rubbed in circles and pressed in when I clenched down on his cock, causing a growl from the back of his throat. I erupted into spasms around him as he thrusted powerfully into me until his own release came meeting me in pure ecstasy.

We spent the next few days in bed naked in between showers and small meals that Jace had delivered. I was enjoying our anniversary and relishing in the love and affection that I knew that I would be missing out on in the next few weeks if not months. Our favorite rock ballad played over the speakers while he made us breakfast. This was our anthem if there was one for our relationship. My hips swayed to the music and leaned into him while the lead singer relayed his anguish and shame as I thought of ours'. How would we deal with our anguish when we were no longer together every day? I knew he loved me. I knew

A Minor Happy Ending

I loved him. I just needed to know if he knew I'd wait. "Babe, do you know how much I love you?" he quickly replied, "How much Sugar?" "More than every breath I take. More than the all the water in the oceans and more than chocolate cake" his smile widened and he said, "more than cake, well shit. This is serious." I smiled and he eased my mind and informed me, "Dyllan, if there was any doubt about the way I feel about you or vise versa. I wouldn't be trying my hardest to make sure you have these memories to keep you with me. None of this would be worth it Dyl, if I came out of this without you. Baby, you are the beginning and the end for me." My heart ached that in a few days I wouldn't have that anymore. "I wish there was another way!" I yelled out causing him to startle almost burning himself on the stove. I looked up at him sheepishly and mouthed I'm sorry. He wrapped his arms around my waste and gave me a reassuring hug while rocking me back and forth. He whispered his endearing words against my head as he turned off the stove. He whispered his adoring words against my neck as he slowly dropped me to the floor and made love to me. Our last couple days at the cabin were spent much like they were in the beginning of our relationship, with random ball room dancing, terribly goofy jokes, and disgustingly awful pick up lines. We cuddled and spoke of fond memories and fun times with our friends. It was six days of perfect. Six days of no worries, no sadness and no responsibilities.

Chapter 32

On day seven, I awoke with a frantic knock on the door. I hopped up to see what the emergency was and opened the door to find Jade standing in front of me with a look of terror on her face. "Hurry up and get dressed! We have to leave now!" she rushed past me, crying and cursing. She began rummaging through drawers and packing my things. Not quite comprehending what she was saying "Wait, what?" I asked groggily. She replied in her panicked tone, "You need to get dressed and tell Jace good bye. They are coming to get him. Dyl, we have to leave. NOW." Jace came in with a look of fear in his eyes, but understanding in his expression, as he frantically began helping her pack my things. "Dyllan! FUCK! Help us, you have to leave!" Jade yelled, but I couldn't move. I just stood there trying to understand what was happening. This couldn't be right I had one more day with him. One more day. My stomach felt like it was in my chest putting pressure on my heart, suffocating me. My legs wouldn't move. I couldn't breathe as I watched the whole scene play out before me like a bad dream. We were going to finally do the right thing. Why now? Why, when we only had one more day? Jace and Jade were running around here like maniacs getting rid of any trace of me here. "Baby move, you have to go!" he said bringing me out of my head. Then the reality of it all hit me like a stack of bricks. NO!

I couldn't. I couldn't. I couldn't. I couldn't do it.

My heart wouldn't take it. I needed him. He was my heart. The air I breathed. I wouldn't make it without him. I got it! Then the dumbest thing I'd ever uttered left my lips, "No, baby let's go! Me and you. We can make a run for it" as he shook his head at me and Jade stared at me like I'd lost my mind. I continued, "I'm not ready baby! I'm not ready for you to go, yet" as the tears streamed down my face and I was feeling that tightening in my chest suffocate me even more, I heard Jade. "Just throw her in the fucking car man!" I was frozen in place as I felt him pick me up and place me in the car as my grip on him tightened. Then, I saw Max gawking at me sympathy with her eyes, when I heard his beautiful reassuring voice tell me, "Baby you have to go, I love you so much and I will contact you as soon as I can." I had a death grip on his shirt and as he pried my hands off of him and I finally had my voice back as I screamed for him, "Please baby don't go, please." He placed one last kiss on my head as a look of resolve appeared on his face and told me he loved me one last time. "Sugar, I got my happy ending because I had you. I love you, Dyllan." I watched him with a feeling of foreboding as he began to walk down the road and out of my life, I thought I heard him hum my song as he disappeared from my view. I thought he was trying to lead them away from me, but it felt like he was leaving for good. I felt a full on panic attack coming on, as I watched him walk away in the rearview mirror of the Century. When I could no longer see him, I whispered words of goodbye.

  Jade headed in the other direction toward home and listened to the pathetic whimpering from me. Even though I was waiting for the "I told ya so" to come, it never did. The long ride home was silent and sullen as I silently blubbered to myself. Jade reached over and grabbed my hand. God I hoped I didn't get her into trouble. I wasn't out of the woods yet, but I couldn't stand not knowing what was happening with Jace. Did they grab him yet? Did they hurt him? What if he got scared and decided that I wasn't worth it? What if they wouldn't let him contact me? I was so pathetic, but I didn't care. I couldn't imagine my life without him. So, I did the only thing I could. I controlled my breathing and withdrew. I didn't want to feel right now since I was sure it'd break me. I couldn't break, not yet. Not here in limbo.

A Minor Happy Ending

Chapter 33

    What? Confusion set in as I sat there imagining my mother's disappointment raining down on my head. Her arms were flailing about and her facial grimacing was something to be desired. I knew she was yelling at me and I knew I should've probably been paying attention since I could've been into some serious trouble. But I wasn't. I was wallowing in the hollow feeling in my chest, waiting to hear from Jace. I just wanted to know that he was okay and that he didn't blame or regret me. If it weren't for me, he wouldn't have missed his appointment and he'd be fine. I truly knew deep down that wasn't true but I found every reason to blame myself because I had no other reasoning about why he had to leave me. I felt like I'd been gutted. Someone stole my sole.

Mom's rant had ceased, not sure if it had because she could tell I wasn't listening or she had finally lost her voice. I hoped it was the latter since I wasn't in the mood for a repeat. For once I really didn't care what Mom had to say. I didn't really think she would have any idea about what I was going through right now.

Jade and Max finally made it over. Mom wasn't happy with them either and it showed by the scowl that they received from her today. They spoke in hushed tones as she scolded them along with me. I still didn't know what she was saying but I was pretty sure it wasn't good. I didn't care. I was an adult. Ultimately it was a bad decision but it was completely worth it.

We sat there for the public scolding session when Officer Joe walked in. Yep there was the face, I was hoping I'd never see. He was disappointed and if I guessed right, maybe hurt. He didn't say anything at first, letting Mom speak her peace which lasted quite a while and then came to kneel in front of me and asked me, "Why didn't you guys ask me for help?" Wow I wasn't expecting that. I looked down, ashamed that I didn't ask the advice of the nice policeman who had treated us well. "Dyllan, look at me" he said more sternly. I looked up with unshed tears clouding my eyes. "We picked him up and he's being processed. He wanted me to tell you he will call you with his one phone call. It probably would've gone on a little longer if he wasn't stupid enough to use his old debit card at the bank. That's how we found him. He withdrew his money from an old account then he gave it to your pretty friends there. We got it all on the bank's camera. When we checked her credit card transactions it showed a purchase for a week at the cabins for the amount he got out of the ATM. When we caught up with him, he said that he was up there alone and that you dumped him days ago when you found out that he had a warrant out for his arrest. Is that true?" Is that true? Well of course, it wasn't true but if that's what Jace's story was, then that's the truth. I nodded as if I'd been listening intently on his every word, but he knew. The look he was giving me told me, he knew. Then the dam broke, "He was going to turn himself in. In two days, he was I swear. We were waiting for our one year anniversary then we were going to do the hard work. He's been working with some lawyer for the last few weeks, trying to fix it. He just didn't want to leave me" the last few words were whispered as I started chastising myself for blabbing, uncontrollable sobs wrecked my whole body as well as my sole. Officer Joe patted my head instead of handcuffing me and stood. He asked my mother to meet him in the hall to talk. My mother returned a few minutes later asking the girls to go home. The disappointed look on her face felt like it was poisoning me. I felt my already broken heart squeeze tighter in my chest. I loved my mom so much, but I didn't and wouldn't regret what I'd done. One day with him was worth it. He was worth everything. She helped me into the shower and into my bed. What she did next surprised me, she began to pet my head, then she began to hum as I drifted off to sleep.

I awoke to my phone ringing, when I heard my mom answer I jolted up because I was afraid she'd hang up. She looked at me with her sad eyes when she said, "Thank you Jace, yes I understand" while nodding and then she said her goodbyes and handed me the phone. I hesitantly pressed the phone to my ear "Hi baby" I said in a raspy voice from too many hours of crying. It was quiet for a moment, then his whispered words come through, "Dyllan,……are you, are you okay?" "I'm missing you like crazy and worried sick." I rushed out and even a little angry as I realized it had been seven hours since I'd heard anything from him. "I know I'm so sorry" he whispered seemingly unable to bring his voice to a normal tone. "Me too." as I began to sob. "Dyllan, don't cry this is hard enough without hearing you break down. Please baby. Please." I tried to stop the crying but found it easier to silent my sounds. The line was silent for a moment when I heard an intake of breath and he blurted, "I talked with

A Minor Happy Ending

Officer Joe, Dyl. He thinks that you will be okay, but my road may not be so easy and I've been thinking. I think while I go down this path that you should go down yours. I've been selfish this whole time, dragging you into this mess. I should've protected you and turned myself in a while ago, but I didn't do that Sugar. I was selfish and didn't pay attention to what you could be losing other than me. I was wrong Dyllan. I'm so sorry baby. While I go down my path to fix myself, I….I think I should do it alone. I'm not dragging you with me anymore. You don't need to hang onto me while you are finishing school and helping your mom." I was shaking my head while the word 'No' repeated itself in my head and I was finding it harder to breathe. "Dyl? Dyl are you there?" A strangled sob escaped my throat and I heard his in the earpiece. "Don't say anything Dyl, just know that I won't contact you anymore and I don't want you to contact me either. Let me fix me and then we will see if our paths cross again." At this point, I no longer heard his words all I felt was panic consuming me causing me to hyperventilate and the sobs came harder. The only thing that I thought that I could do to stop the pain was hang up. So I did. I curled into the fetal position on my bed and sobbed. I heard the phone ring again and my mother answered and I heard her loving yet stern tone, she saved for me when she was disappointed. I heard her finally say fine as the phone was pressed to my ear and I heard a frustrated man growl in my ear, "I fucking love you Dyllan, you'll always be mine. I fucking love you. We may not of had our happy ending, but there will always be a piece of you that is mine and you will always own my heart." Then the line went dead and all I could think of was that he left me. I couldn't believe he left me. We had a plan.

A Minor Happy Ending

Epilogue

Present Day

"WOW, that's pretty fucked up mom! That guy sounds like trouble" my daughter says bravely. "Kasey Jade! Watch your mouth" I say with a little sarcasm. She smiles as she cuddles into my lap as I pet her hair. "Well it is!" she says knowing that I firmly agree. I nod my head and explain, "Well, that's why I told you that story. I wanted you to know what an omitted truth did to me one time, but I also wanted to get the point across that it doesn't mean that he doesn't love you baby girl. It just means that people mess up. They lie out of fear. They get jealous. They fight, but it doesn't mean that the love isn't there. Another point of my story is that sometimes love isn't enough to make it work, but in some cases it is."   "So, you're saying I should forgive him for not telling me that his ex girlfriend has been calling him and trying to get him to meet up with her?" she asks with vehemence. "Did he?" I ask. "No, not yet." She says while dropping her eyes to the ground and shaking her head. "What says he will, Kase? He probably didn't want to upset you and…" when I hear the doorbell. I jump up when my husband yells. "I got it." I head to the door anyway and walk up behind my husband to find a rather sullen-looking young man with red-rimmed eyes and a hesitant smile. "Is Kase here?" My husband with his unknowing smile responds, "ya sure, Kase, Jason's here! Come on in man." I nod at Jason as he hesitantly walks in the door with his hands shoved deep into his pockets and his shoulders slump. I point to the room where my equally stubborn and lovely daughter awaits. She looks up to see him and tears fall down her cheeks as I turn to give her some privacy, I find my handsome husband looking on with concern. He looks to me for confirmation and I nod. I use my eyes to direct him in the other room. When we enter our bedroom, he doesn't waste time wrapping me in his arms while questioning what is going on. "Lovers spat?" he says and I affirm that it was and we agree to give them some time to work things through.

As per usual when we are alone, his hands begin to roam and I respond immediately. I am wet and ready when his hands reach my sex, he groans his approval. Thank god I went commando under my yoga pants! "God, you're always so wet for me. Baby, do you know how sexy that is?" a moan escapes my throat as he slowly circles my clit building the pressure while he kissing and licking my neck

A Minor Happy Ending

and ears. I feel my body being lowered to the bed and him growl in my ear, "Only gets better baby. Every day gets better. I love you more and find you sexier every fucking day." I feel my orgasm rip through me when his sexy words reverberate through my ears. He peels all of his clothes off of his body revealing the tattoo over his heart with mine as well as both of our children's names written with chains and locks surrounding our names symbolizing our undying connection. I always place my hand over his heart as we make love to remind him that his heart belongs to me as mine does to him as he places his hands over mine. When he finally enters me and fills me full of not only his hardness but his love. He always makes love to me like it will be our last time. He always tells me that he loves me every day and he always lets me keep a little piece of myself that I left a long time ago. As I remember how lucky I am to have married the most loyal, kind and honest man, who had loved and honored me all of our marriage, I am so proud to be his wife.

When we reach our orgasm together this time, my emotion from this day has brought me to tears. Happy tears. He holds me, rocking me back and forth as he hums in my ear. He pulls me away and looks down into my eyes and as he opens his mouth to speak, the phone rings.

"Hello" he answers while his other arm is wrapped protectively around me. He continues, "ya…. ya she's right here." He hands me the phone and wraps his free arm around me to help comfort me. "Hello" I say into the phone when I hear the familiar chipper voice on the other line, "Hi, pickles." I smile and answer, "Hi, Papa Joe how are you? And how's mom?" he laughs and says, "a tiger, I can't keep her hands off of me." I laugh at his terrible joke while he continues, "oh ya, I'm serious. I may not make it until my birthday Sunday. Hey, that's why I was calling. Your mom wanted to know if Kasey was bringing "the boyfriend"." I quickly reply, "oh dad you never like any of her boyfriends. Glad you didn't meet all of my mine." I look up into curious eyes and hold my finger up to my mouth. "Let me ask her." I quickly dress and head toward the living room where we left the two when I see my baby girl with her eyes so blindly full of love and devotion and a young man mirroring her expression, trace each other's lips with their fingers as soft words are spoken. I see a small smile appear across her lips and he leans in to kiss her. I smile and whisper in the phone, "Yep, he'll be there." After we say our good-byes I feel strong warm arms wrap around me, reminding me that he is my home. Then he coughs rather loudly not only bringing me out of my head but the kids out of theirs. Such an over protective father. Jason blushes and Kasey scoffs, "Nice dad!" We chuckle at

A Minor Happy Ending

our daughter's remark. "We are going to go, I'll text ya when I know what's up" I nod and address Jason, "My dad's birthday party is Sunday. We'd love for you to come." He looks to Kasey for reassurance that it's okay with her and she nods. She looks at me with appreciative eyes. "That'd be great. Thanks" he says sounding relieved. She smiles her Hollywood smile while grabbing his hand and leading him off to his car. My handsome husband looks down to me with his sexy crooked grin and says, "Do you think she'll have her happy ending, Mrs. Harvey?" as he places his lips in the small of my neck, I whisper, "I hope so babe, but I sure as hell have gotten mine."

The End

Dedications

To my beautiful family, you are the inspiration for everything that I do. You are the center of my universe. Baby, there isn't a "book boyfriend" out there who could compare to you. You are the best thing to ever happen to me and I'm grateful you chose to spend your life with me. Thank you for believing in me and giving me the confidence to follow one of my many dreams. Loolee and Smelly, you make every day better and I'm so thankful that I have you two in my world. You make it a brighter place every day (even when you leave your laundry on the floor)...

To my CCC TEAM, thank you for giving me the encouragement and the confidence to publish my little story. Thank you for helping me achieve a dream of mine. No one could've asked for better friends. All of you are amazing and it's a pleasure to call you my second family.

A Minor Happy Ending

To my original family, you've made me what I am today. My endless drive and bottomless heart come from you. Love you.

To my Now & Then Forever Friends, you are always going to be inspiration for me. I'm blessed to have a group of friends that span a lifetime. You are the best friends a girl could have and thank you for having my back and supporting me whether I made good decisions or not. You are all priceless. Love you.

To my Cathy & Kathy, who always have my back and remind me of what's the most important. You two are very dear to my heart and I'm so lucky I have you ladies in my life. Love you.

If you want to know how Dyllan and Jace found each other again, stay tuned..........

A Happily Ever After is coming soon.

And maybe Nick may have a tale of his own coming your way.

To stay connected to Shaan Ranae, follow her on FB and Twitter

@Shaan_Ranae on Twitter Visit http://twitter.com/@shaan_ranae

Author Shaan Ranae on Facebook . Visit http://facebook.com/ShaanRanae

Made in the USA
Columbia, SC
11 June 2017